WITHDRAWN

10/18/18

The
INJUSTICE
COLLECTORS

The
INJUSTICE COLLECTORS

by

Louis Auchincloss

HOUGHTON MIFFLIN COMPANY · BOSTON
The Riverside Press Cambridge

mnr95-388

MONROE COUNTY COMMUNITY COLLEGE LIBRARY
Monroe, Michigan

SECOND PRINTING   R

COPYRIGHT, 1949, 1950, BY LOUIS AUCHINCLOSS
ALL RIGHTS RESERVED INCLUDING THE RIGHT TO REPRODUCE THIS
BOOK OR PARTS THEREOF IN ANY FORM
𝔗𝔥𝔢 𝔕𝔦𝔳𝔢𝔯𝔰𝔦𝔡𝔢 𝔓𝔯𝔢𝔰𝔰
CAMBRIDGE · MASSACHUSETTS
PRINTED IN THE U.S.A.

3 3131 00055 9975

CONTENTS

The Miracle 1

Maud 29

The Fall of a Sparrow 69

Finish, Good Lady 93

The Unholy Three 119

The Ambassadress 151

The Edification of Marianne 187

Greg's Peg 215

ACKNOWLEDGMENT

M<small>AUD</small>" and "Finish, Good Lady" first appeared in the Atlantic Monthly, "The Ambassadress" in Town & Country. The lines from "East Coker" are reprinted from *Four Quartets*, copyright, 1943, by T. S. Eliot and the lines from *The Cocktail Party* are copyright, 1950, by T. S. Eliot. Both selections are used by permission of Harcourt, Brace and Company, Inc.

AUTHOR'S NOTE

I CAME ACROSS the term "injustice collectors" in "The Battle of the Conscience" by Dr. Edmund Bergler. It is a term which he uses to describe neurotics who continually and unconsciously construct situations in which they are disappointed or mistreated. This broad definition is followed by a more detailed description of the psychological process involved, in which he points out, among other things, that these persons are seeking unconscious masochistic pleasure. I do not purport to use the term in Dr. Bergler's exact medical sense, but in a wider sense to describe people who are looking for injustice, even in a friendly world, because they suffer from a hidden need to feel that this world has wronged them. Turning the idea over, one begins to speculate if punishment and injustice are not *always* more sought after than seeking, not only for such a reason as self-pity, but for other reasons, both lower and higher. Is not the neurotic or the maladjusted or the unconventional or even the saint in some fashion the magnet that attracts the very disaster that he may appear to be seeking to avoid? Such, anyway, was the germ that grew into this collection of stories. That a character's undoing or rejection may be the result of his own course of action is hardly surprising, but it may be significant that he has chosen, not only the course, but the result to which it leads. I do not attempt to go into the *why* of all this. That is for the psychiatrist, or possibly the novelist, but not necessarily for the short story writer. The latter may content himself with symptoms rather than causes.

L. A.

THE MIRACLE

Unlike are we, unlike, O princely Heart!
Unlike our uses and our destinies.
Our ministering two angels look surprise
On one another, as they strike athwart
Their wings in passing.

—Elizabeth Barrett Browning

THE MIRACLE

It was my sister, Rosa, who made me go that night to the Duntons'. She was well aware that, when I came to stay with her in her big stone castellated horror in Anchor Harbor, it was for the rest and the Maine air, but there were certain invitations that she could be very firm about, particularly ones where she thought feelings might otherwise be hurt. For Rosa, as large and square in feature as she was gentle and kind in disposition, was one of those adored old maids who must see the best in everyone, and I don't suppose there was a person on the peninsula, either of the village or of the summer crowd, for whom she had not at one time or other done a considerable favor. When I had made, in late middle age, the fortune that as a young man I had cared so much about making and had bought back for Rosa our old family place in Anchor Harbor, with all its lawns and gardens, it had only, as it turned out, been to provide a larger headquarters for her beneficence. But I had to draw the line somewhere, and I tried to draw it with the Duntons.

"They would never have me in their house before I made my money," I pointed out to her as we sat, after breakfast, on the terrace that looked over the lawn to the ocean. "They're the baldest kind of snobs. I hear their food is the worst in the community and that they don't pay their servants. Really, Rosa. There *are* limits."

But Rosa, when embarked on an errand of good will, was not so easily to be put off. Her fingers were working busily to tuck in a loose braid of gray hair that kept escaping from the knot on top of her head.

"Alice Dunton is not really a snob," she explained. "She's only pathetic. She was never that way before George went through her money. Now she has all these children, and she's scared, poor creature. Entertaining is her way of keeping her head up. And she has to spread a very little money over a very expensive summer."

I snorted.

"And a very little brain over a large ambition," I said.

Rosa eyed me disapprovingly.

"You've still got that chip on your shoulder, Philip," she said, shaking her head. "Even now, when you're the most important person up here. You should have got it off after all these years. You can afford to be generous. And the Duntons are really perfectly all right. When you get to know them."

I threw my hands in the air.

"When *you* get to know them, Rosa," I retorted. "Leave me out of it, I beg you."

But there was something in what Rosa said, and I knew it. Our parents had been summer residents of Anchor

Harbor who had become, thanks to the panic of 1907, "natives"; they had had to sell the big house that Rosa now occupied and move into a small one in the village. I had been brought up there and had suffered from being, so to speak, neither fish nor fowl; I had had to endure the embarrassed condescension of the club members and the guarded friendliness of the village people. It made me distant now with all of them, and although I spent every August with Rosa it was more for the satisfaction of seeing her re-established and feeling that I had accomplished this than for renewing my acquaintance with the old community.

"You needn't get to know them, dear," Rosa said firmly, ending the argument. "All you need to do is dine there. Once."

Of course, I went, and, of course, it was as bad as I supposed. Occasionally I get tired of being right. The Duntons maintained an atmosphere of rather haggard cordiality in an old shingle house on the ocean drive that was literally falling to pieces. On Sunday nights, apparently, the friends of both generations of the family foregathered in the dining room with the spotted ceiling and the faded tapestry chairs for a buffet supper that was as unappetizing as it was meager. Mr. Dunton, a mild fat gullible man who had slipped softly into alcoholism and inertia, was generally ignored by the others. His wife, on the other hand, was as strident as he was negative; her dyed red hair and square face bobbed from group to group. She made a great fuss over me when I arrived, but not, I will confess, quite as much fuss as I had thought she would make.

"Mr. Ives is what we call a 'tycoon,'" she explained to the group around her. "We're terribly honored that he has come."

They all grinned at me and at each other, and I moved

away from them after Rosa. I had grown accustomed to the invariable tribute to my financial success, and I even rather missed it when it was withheld, but I preferred it with some degree of subtlety in its expression. Mrs. Dunton's crudeness disgusted me. I nodded briefly and steered Rosa to a little table in the corner.

"We can't, Philip!" she whispered in alarm. "You've got to talk to the others."

"You got me into this," I said firmly, "and you're not going to desert me. Now sit down. I shall get two plates of lettuce salad. When we have finished them we will go home and have a decent dinner."

I would not yield, and poor Rosa had to be a sport. When we were settled, as unobtrusively as possible, in a corner, I looked around the big room to take in the full horror of it. There were people sitting at little tables like ours; there were young people sitting on the floor, and, in the embrasure of the bay window, there was a larger table at the end of which sat a girl who looked very much like Mrs. Dunton. She had small, silly features in a pale, expressionless face, and her blonde hair was elaborately waved. I pointed her out to Rosa.

"A daughter?"

"Isabella. The oldest. She's pretty, isn't she?"

I looked at Rosa with discouragement.

"No, dear," I said, "she is *not* pretty. And not far from thirty, I should imagine. Is she still unmarried?"

"Yes."

"I suppose she'll have the deuce of a time finding a husband."

Even Rosa seemed to agree that this might be the case.

"Do you suppose," I persisted, "that she has any idea of how perfectly dreadful this party is?"

For once Rosa surprised me. I had expected that she would deny that the party was dreadful.

"I think she may," she said, following my gaze across the room. "Poor Isabella."

Something in this unexpected falling away of Rosa's optimism made me curious to know if Miss Dunton really *did* know. Would it be possible, after all, for a girl to have lived as she had lived without some sense of the horror of it? I examined her more closely and tried to imagine what could be going on under those stiff little curled locks and behind those small, restless black eyes. It was not an intelligent face, yet I had a sense, conveyed by the way in which her eyes moved back and forth and up and down, of somebody imprisoned behind the hard white of her powder and trying, in a hopeless, clumsy way, to clamber out. That somebody was always slipping back; the effort, if effort it was, was purely perfunctory. Surely she could not have been unaware of the rudeness of the butler who was pouring the lamentable wine or of the sorry figure that her father cut as the only person who was drinking it. Surely she must have felt some pang at her own frozen position amid the empty chatter of her married contemporaries. What, then, could be the energy that kept her going through the forms of being a débutante so long after she had ceased to be one, making small talk with men who were already tired of their own wives and searching for diversion very different from what poor Isabella could offer? Our eyes suddenly met, and I was shocked to realize that we were staring at each other. We nodded and promptly looked away from each other, but in that single instant I had felt a communication across the room.

"Rosa," I said, turning abruptly to my sister, "you're right. She *does* know."

Rosa looked startled.

"Knows what?"

"But, of course. I see it," I continued enthusiastically. "The poor girl's desperate. She's waiting for a miracle."

She tried to follow me.

"A miracle?"

I looked again at Isabella, this time more furtively.

"Exactly." I was quite sure of it now. "In the form of a handsome young man who will be suddenly and inexplicably ardent. She won't know why, and *he* won't know why. That will be the miracle."

Rosa shrugged her shoulders as she looked around the room.

"And she'll meet him here?" she asked.

"Exactly. Between the courses." I glanced disdainfully at the sideboard. "Amid the platitudes. Suddenly and unbelievably. There he will be."

But my sister was not one to indulge in such flights of the fancy.

"How could she think so?" she demanded. "When she's Isabella Dunton?"

"Oh, I don't say she *thinks* so. There's nothing rational about it. It's a faith."

Rosa laughed.

"You practical men of affairs," she said. "You certainly go overboard when you leave Wall Street."

When I turned back to Isabella I saw that the men at the younger table had risen and were gathered about the sideboard for the next course. Isabella was now seated alone, and I could see that she was watching somebody. This was the more noticeable as her eyes, for the first time since I had been watching her, had ceased their roving. They were fixed, quite obviously, on a particular object, and I thought I could make out, in the very expressionlessness of her features, an air of covert relaxation, of almost guilty repose, as though she had been looking forward to this little break in the rigors of her pointless discipline. I had the curious feeling, after the first encounter of our eyes, that we had established a means of communication between ourselves, and when she glanced again in my direction, without actually looking at me, I felt a little stir of excitement at the realization that what she was telling me was that I *was* right. The miracle had, in fact, occurred. I shared her amazement and her fear; I found myself smiling at her, even though her face was now averted from mine, smiling with the sympathy of our joint sense of the impossibility of what was happening to her. I allowed my eyes to follow the direction of hers, and just before they had focused on the doorway where somebody was standing, I knew, in a horrible second and with the searing realization that I had known it from the beginning, who the young man would be.

2

Alex, the young man at whom I had seen Isabella staring, was my son. He was, indeed, even more than that to me, for he was my only child. I had been married, long before, but my wife had left me, ostensibly for another man but actually, I have always thought, because I was not doing well enough at the time. It has given me a grim satisfaction through the years to continue, quite voluntarily, to support her and her second husband and their several children out of the proceeds of a fortune which she never thought I would make. I have never pretended to myself that this was generous on my part; I know my own motives and satisfactions too well. And then, it is only fair to add, I kept Alex away from her; Rosa and I brought the boy up ourselves and never thought it necessary so much as to mention his mother's name.

I should admit right off that Alex was the center of my life; I cared for him with a possessiveness that cost me a daily effort to hide. I was afraid of the emotion and the prospect of my own loneliness upon his leaving me, but he was twenty-two and I could not expect that he would stay unmarried much after his graduation from Harvard. He was, after all, the only heir to my fortune, in addition to which he was, to me, anyway, the handsomest young man in the world. He was very pale and romantic looking; he had long dark hair and intense black eyes and said very little, but what he did say seemed always to be sincere. He had a truculent but loyal nature, and I allowed myself to form a picture of him as the misunderstood and vaguely misanthropic hero of a Byron poem. Of course, I could see that he was physically too short for the part and that he preferred engineering to poetry, but as long as he gave himself no airs it was up to me to supply them for him. He was a remarkably good boy, devoted to his Aunt Rosa and very respectful to me, and I tried never to betray to him that I was hurt by his failure to reciprocate the intensity of my concern for him. After all, I deserved it. I was a doting father.

I sat frozen now as I watched him cross the room to sit by Isabella. Obviously ardent, he leaned forward in his chair to say what I imagined were passionate things. Isabella was listening to him with a frightened, twitching expression. She kept nibbling at olives and glancing at her mother. I could imagine what he must be saying about the party. Surely he must have found it humiliating to be in the clutches of a girl whose family stood so brazenly, so ludicrously, for everything he despised. For Alex was honest, honest in everything. And that girl, that impossible girl, what could she be thinking of? It was against nature; it was against all that was holy. When I could stand it no longer I got up abruptly and left without even saying good night to the Duntons. Rosa followed me. I assumed that she had seen what I had seen. She knew me, at any rate, too well to discuss it.

At home I sat alone in the library leaving the door ajar so that I could see Alex when he came in. It was, of course, impossible for me to do anything but play solitaire in my agitated state of mind. It was after one o'clock when I heard his key in the door, and I had played more than twenty games. He must have seen the light in the study for he came in and sat down in the chair opposite my desk. There was just the trace of a smile on his face.

"How are you, Dad?" he asked.

"As well as can be expected. After that dreadful party."

He nodded, his large eyes fixed upon me.

"It was pretty bad, wasn't it?"

"Unspeakable," I snapped, looking up at him. "The Duntons are quite impossible. Of course, you can go where you like, but you would be doing me a very great favor if you never went there again."

His expression did not change.

"Yet you went there yourself, Dad."

"Your aunt tricked me into it," I said impatiently. "It will not happen again, I can assure you."

"You didn't like my being with Isabella Dunton, did you, Dad?" he asked me. His eyes looked through me as he said this, and there was still a faint smile on his lips, a smile that seemed to be serving as an expression of neutrality until I should give him his cue.

"I did not."

"You condemn Isabella because of her parents," he said in the same level tone. "You don't know her."

"I concede that."

"You don't know," he pursued more feelingly, "the beautiful side of Isabella. Hidden under all the foolishness. You haven't given her a chance, Dad."

I could not face the intensity of his expression, and I looked down at the heavy gold paperweight that my fingers were resting on. My voice trembled.

"And why, if you please," I demanded, "should I be obligated to give Isabella Dunton a chance?"

"Because I'm going to marry her."

My hands went abruptly to my ears. I got up and walked to the fireplace. I was dizzy.

"You're mad," was all I could say.

"Possibly."

"She's years older than you," I protested wildly. "She's not right for you in any way! She's nothing but a — cipher. It may not be her fault," I added hastily as I saw his expression, "but, my poor boy, there you are. She's stuck in that muddy life. And oh, Alex! Think of her mother!" At the thought of Mrs. Dunton my discretion deserted me. "My God!" I exclaimed, almost to myself, "I haven't brought you up to satisfy the social ambitions of Alice Dunton!"

Alex had followed me to the fireplace and had placed a restraining hand on my elbow.

"But I love her, Dad," he protested. "I know how you feel about Mrs. Dunton, but you can't imagine how I feel about Isabella. And it won't be for the Duntons. I'm going to take Isabella away from all that. We want to live in California. We won't even want any money. Oh, Dad." I felt the pressure of his fingers. "Try to see it our way."

I turned and looked into his pleading eyes. Never in his life that I could remember had he appealed to me before. Never could I have imagined that I would have refused him anything. But my mind had become a hell of smirking Duntons, and I was no longer myself. The picture of their taking him off, to a cottage in California, cut the last strand that tied me to any hope of reasonableness.

"See it your way!" I almost shouted. "See you shackled to that idiot of a girl to satisfy the crazy ambitions of her mother! Do you think I'm out of my mind?"

"I'm sorry, Dad." He had turned very pale. "I had hoped you wouldn't feel that way." And he left the room, leaving me to the misery of my remorse and the sad, sick conviction that I was not going to repent.

3

The next two weeks were of a constraint that can be imagined. Alex stayed on at home, but he went out to almost all of his meals, and when he and I met we only nodded. He had wanted to move to a hotel, or even to the Duntons', but Rosa had induced him not to do so. She had had to use, as I discovered later, all her influence with him to keep him from hurting me by so open an abandonment, and she had guaranteed, on her part, that she would bring me around to some sort of compliance. Poor Alex was not so idealistic as to ignore how vital a trump card I could be to him in dealing with the Duntons. When Rosa told me that Isabella had refused to elope with him I had my first glimmering of hope.

"She's not, then, swept off her feet," I said sarcastically. "Nothing, I imagine, but a mink coat would accomplish that."

"You're entirely wrong," Rosa said heatedly. Rosa, to my disgust, had been carried away by the romance of the situation. "She's simply being an obedient daughter. After all, they've hardly let her out of their sight since she was born."

"Some thirty-odd years ago."

"Really, Philip," Rosa protested, "I don't know what's got into you. I've never seen you this way. That girl is not thirty yet. She may not be the most attractive thing in the world, and Alice Dunton may not be the mother-in-law that you or I would have picked for Alex, but you go on as if he were marrying some thing off the streets."

"Which I would vastly prefer."

Rosa looked at me with real severity. The pince-nez that perched on the thin bridge of her long nose quivered as she spoke.

"I've known Isabella all her life," she said, "and she's a dear, *sweet* girl. I don't know what sort of a princess you expect for your Alex, but if you keep on acting this way you're going to have a lonely old age, Philip Ives. I'm warning you!"

Even Rosa, however, would not have succeeded in putting across her plan for another meeting between the Duntons and myself had I not anticipated results from it that she did not foresee. I had finally told Alex that if he would put off his marriage for a year I would withdraw my objections. It had been a desperate gamble, but, after all, what had I to lose? He could, of course, have married her at any time. He had agreed to this, having, in any event, another year of Harvard, and I told Rosa that she might ask the Duntons for tea. I stipulated that afterwards they should meet me in another room, accompanied by Isabella and Alex, for a general discussion of affairs. I also stipulated that Rosa was not to be present. She looked at me skeptically.

"If you have any tricks in mind, Philip Ives," she told me, "you'd better watch your step. Alex will tell me all about it afterwards."

When they came Rosa gave them tea on the terrace while I paced up and down in the garden. Afterwards I received them, not in the study which implied, I thought, all of the paraphernalia of a financial settlement, but in the big French parlor. There was a stiff, brisk shaking of hands after which I took up my stand by the fireplace with Mr. and Mrs. Dunton each seated on a sofa on either side and Alex and Isabella facing each other on little gilt chairs. Isabella said nothing; she sat with her hands in her lap and her eyes on the floor.

"We're here, I understand, Mr. and Mrs. Dunton," I began in a distant and businesslike tone, "to discuss this purported engagement between our children. You will forgive me, I trust, if I tell you frankly that I am not even going to pretend to be pleased. There is nothing, I assure you, the least personal in my attitude. I know that your Isabella is a charming and excellent young lady. But I will not conceal from you that I had hoped that Alex would not marry for at least five years. However, I am not one to oppose the inevitable."

This little speech was followed by the rather clamorous sympathy of both Mr. and Mrs. Dunton. They agreed with me, it appeared, as to the inadvisability of early marriages. Even for their Isabella, I gathered, this moment, long dreaded in their parental hearts, was considered premature. But like me they were stoics. They, too, faced with resolution the prospect of losing their child.

After a proper exchange of civilities Mr. Dunton, with an embarrassed little chuckle, started on the subject that I had been waiting for.

"What's done is done, as they say," he said with false heartiness, "and the old folks will have to swallow it. Isn't that about the gist of it, Mr. Ives? I guess it is. It's better, as the good saint put it, to marry than burn. Yes, indeed. But marriage, I'm told, is more than a ceremony. We can't expect these youngsters to live on air, can we?" Here there was another chuckle which was not echoed by the rest of us. "My wife always accuses me of being too forthright," he continued more briskly, "and I confess it's one of my faults. So here goes. What do you expect to do for these young people, Mr. Ives? In the way of a settlement and all? Oh, I know about gift taxes and that sort of thing," he added hastily as he saw my frown. "I mean just a rough idea."

He looked up at me in boldness and embarrassment. It was not, I was sure, the first time that he had been through such a scene.

"I'm afraid, Mr. Dunton, that you misconceive the situation," I said coldly. "Any inquiries as to my son's ability to support your daughter should be addressed to him. I have made none, you will note, as to what you are planning to settle on Isabella."

Isabella's parents exchanged glances. Then her father turned to me, with a smile that seemed to deprecate the formality of my approach, his hands held out in a gesture that suggested that surely, among friends, such things could be worked out.

"You are very European in your thinking, I see, Mr. Ives," he said blandly. "I like that myself. I was educated in England and, before the war, my wife and I went almost every summer to France. But, after all, here we are in America. When in Rome, you know, and all that. Surely a fine young man like your son isn't going to go around demanding doweries." He beamed from Alex to me. "He'd probably be ashamed to touch a penny of Isabella's money. Isn't that right, son?"

Alex nodded vigorously. But I had the upper hand, and I intended to keep it.

"I'm glad you say that, Mr. Dunton," I said, "because I am entirely in accord. As you say, we are in America. I believe there is a feeling here that each generation should make its own way. I am sure that Alex will work hard and well to support his wife. I made my way. He, I have no doubt, will make his."

Mrs. Dunton, who had been listening to me with the wide eyes of a single and outraged point of view, now burst into the conversation.

"You mean you will do nothing for these young people?" she demanded.

"You might put it that way," I answered, nodding. "Of course, sickness and actual need are other matters. And I'm perfectly willing to discuss a moderate allowance until Alex gets on his feet. But as to setting him up in the station in life that you, perhaps, might deem fitting for your daughter, that I have no idea of doing."

Mrs. Dunton threw her hands in the air. She was dealing, it was clear, with a lunatic.

"But how can a young man make any money these days?" she protested. "With taxes and everything? It was different when you were young, Mr. Ives. Anyone could pile up a fortune then." She paused, considering, perhaps, the implications of her remark as they affected Mr. Dunton. "If he had any luck," she added by way of qualification, and then, suddenly seeing her way clear down the broad highway of a new fallacy, conceived on the instant, she continued: "I think it's the *duty* of people who made money in the easy days to help out the young people. I really do!"

"It's a duty, the execution of which I will have to leave to you, Mrs. Dunton."

"Daddy!" Alex protested.

"I've had great losses, Mr. Ives," she said proudly. "I think it unworthy that you, with a recent fortune, should sneer at our old families."

I bowed.

"I was not sneering, Mrs. Dunton," I said with dignity. "I know nothing of your affairs. Nor would I have the impertinence to inquire."

She stared at me, baffled.

"I suppose you will leave them something in your will?" she asked. "Or do your principles require that the poor children be cut off entirely?"

"The terms of my will, Mrs. Dunton," I answered, "will not be known until my death. That event might occur at any moment. We live, of course, on sufferance. But I think I should tell you that the average age attained by my grandparents was eighty-one and that I have not yet finished my fifty-fifth year."

Mrs. Dunton had now worked herself into a frame of mind very different from that in which she had come to call. She had come as a suppliant, slightly embarrassed, perhaps, not at what she herself thought of her rôle, but at what I, a person unversed in the world, might be thinking of it. She would leave, however, magnificently, riding out on the billowing wave of her offended generosity.

"I was told," she said rising and signaling her husband to do the same, "that I might expect such treatment from you. That you had no understanding of our world at Anchor Harbor." Her bosom seemed to fill as she talked and her hands, folded together, were tucked to her waist like the buckle of a belt. "I answered that I never judged people on the basis of gossip. But now, Mr. Ives, I have found out for myself. There can be no further talk of marriage between our children. I am sorry, Alex, for your sake," she added to my son. "For you I would have overlooked a lot. But not everything. No, not quite. Come my dear," she said to her husband, "come Isabella. We're taking up Mr. Ives' *valuable* time."

She turned to the door, followed by her obedient husband and daughter, and was going out when Alex cried:

"Isabella! What do *we* care?"

She shook her head several times in rapid succession.

"Please," she said. *"Please!"* And she hurried out after her parents, leaving Alex and me alone in the big yellow and gold room with all the chairs. Alex stood by a window, looking out at the lawn. His hands were in his pockets.

"Alex."

There was no indication that he had heard me.

"I have to keep pinching my arm," I went on, "to make myself realize that the scene which we have just witnessed could have taken place in the middle of the twentieth century."

"You seem to have handled it well enough," he said coldly. "Perhaps you don't belong in this century."

I was stung by his tone.

"What would you have had me do, Alex?" I demanded. "Give in to them? Should I have *bought* you a wife? Is that what you wanted?"

"No, no." He turned around and sat down heavily on a little gilt chair. He looked tired and hopeless. "I wouldn't have wanted her. Under those conditions. But the way she sat there!" He shook his head sadly. "As if it were the most usual thing in the world! Can you beat it?" His voice rose. "She sat there while her old bitch of a mother tried to sell her off! Without even blinking!"

My success was gratifying, perhaps too gratifying.

"I hope you understand now, Alex," I said more gently, "why I insisted that you and Isabella be present. A parent has a lot of painful duties. But that, to date, has been the most painful of mine."

He looked up at me for the first time and seemed to hear what I was saying.

"Difficult?" he said, and his voice was bitter. "Why I don't suppose you've ever had such a good time in your life!"

"Alex!"

"Standing there," he continued in a voice of contempt, "and pretending to be the exponent of Americanism! How you *hate* them!" He looked savagely around the room. "That's why you're here. To make them all eat crow. And I'm nothing but a pawn in your filthy scheme!"

I could only gape at him.

"Alex, you know I didn't mean what I said to them," I protested desperately. "You know that I don't have a penny that's not yours. You can marry the girl today if you want. I only wanted to show you what they were like. That was all. Really that was all."

"I don't want your money," he retorted brutally. "Or anything else from you. I just want to get the hell out of here!"

Saying which, he flung out of the room. I was beyond resentment. I sat there, looking at the afternoon sunlight that slanted over the rhododendron bushes outside the windows and facing a world where the Duntons and Alex were allied against me.

4

Rosa, as usual, came to the rescue and stopped Alex from walking out on me entirely. She took him, I gathered, very much to task for his treatment of me and even induced him, morosely, to apologize. She then packed him off for the rest of the summer on a fishing trip to Canada and allowed me the pleasure of ordering him a large supply of expensive equipment.

The trip seemed to be the thing. He wrote long, introspective letters to Rosa, parts of which she read aloud to me, but it was obvious, even from these, that he *was* fishing and catching, we gathered, quite a lot of fish. After three weeks he even sent me a postcard with a noncommittal scrawl about the scenery, and I felt with elation that I might be on the threshold of forgiveness.

I did not, needless to say, see any more of the Duntons, and I was just allowing myself to hope that the episode, all things considered, had been astutely handled and finally closed when I had my unfortunate conversation with Isabella on the cliff walk.

I could go all the way from Rosa's house to the swimming club along the cliff walk, and I used to take this stroll every morning at noon. It involved passing between the sea and the backs of the big houses along the main street, and I enjoyed their wide sloping lawns with the sprinklers idly turning and the occasional gardener dragging a hose or pushing a wheelbarrow. There was a peace in this particular view of them that their owners never conveyed. A few weeks after Alex's departure, as I was passing the Duntons' house I saw Isabella standing alone on the edge of the path. She was looking out at the sea and did not notice me. When I paused, however, she turned, and I could see that she had been crying.

"I beg your pardon," I said, taken aback.

She gave her head a little shake and then smiled at me. It was a rather forced smile.

"Good morning!" she exclaimed. "Are you walking to the club? What a lovely morning it is!"

I nodded.

"May I go along with you?" she asked. "I was just on my way. I always tell Mummie: 'How can you even get into a car on a day like this?' Can *you* understand it, Mr. Ives? I can't."

We walked on together, Isabella chatting about the lovely weather and the tennis and the party at the club the following Saturday night as if nothing under the sun had ever occurred between us. I marveled at the steady flow of her triviality; it seemed to fill the channels of her existence and overflow the borders, and one could not but wonder at the nature of the pumping force that kept it coming. I noticed how pale her cheeks were and how dark the shadows under her eyes.

"I heard from Alex this morning," I said.

"Oh?" She paused with a polite air of curiosity. "And how is dear Alex?"

"He's in Quebec," I said shortly. "Fishing and feeling

sorry for himself. But he'll get over it, I imagine."

"Oh, I'm sure he will!" she said eagerly. "He's so young!"

Something in her voice provoked me unreasonably. I stopped and looked at her. Politely, she stopped too.

"He's not as young as that makes him sound," I said. "He is, after all, a man. If arrangements could have been made to your parents' satisfaction, I take it you would not have turned him down?"

She looked agitated.

"No," she said. "I suppose not."

"You had some feeling for him, then?"

"Oh, I think all of us girls have a feeling for Alex," she answered with a fatuous smile. "Yes, indeed! He's such a handsome boy. And he plays such divine tennis. Why, Mummie was saying — "

I was suddenly furious. I stepped forward and grabbed her hands in mine.

"I don't give a damn what your mummie said," I interrupted roughly. "Is that all you cared about him? God!" I let her hands drop and stared into her terrified eyes. "What right does a person like you have to play with other people's feelings?"

She stared back at me, trembling.

"What is it you want, Mr. Ives?"

"Want?" I repeated in disgust. "I want to know what a girl like you is made of."

To my sudden dismay I saw that her eyes were again full of tears.

"You're so hard," she said, looking miserably down at the grass. "You didn't want me to marry Alex, and I didn't. And now you're angry with me for not caring enough. Is that fair, Mr. Ives?"

"It was *your* decision, wasn't it," I demanded, "to let

him go?"

I had a sudden sensation that she was about to collapse, and I reached out instinctively to support her elbow.

"Wasn't it?" I repeated tensely.

"I knew you'd never have it," she said in a strangled tone. "I knew it when you were looking at me that night at dinner. I knew you were right, too," she said with a sudden desperate sob. "What had I ever done to deserve a beautiful boy like that? I know what people say about me. I know that I'm 'poor Isabella.' 'Poor sad Isabella.'" She looked at me with resentment, an expression I had not seen on her face before. It made her look crumpled and gray. "I couldn't tell him I didn't love him, could I? Would anyone have believed that? Would they?"

I could only stare at her, appalled.

"What do you think a girl like me goes through," she continued bitterly, "when a boy like that wants to marry her? Nothing? I may not be smart the way you are, Mr. Ives, but at least I know what I can do and what I can't do. And I knew I could never be what Alex thinks I am. I could never live up to him at all. It's not that I wouldn't go to California with him. It's that he'd hate me when he got me there. But could I tell *him* that, Mr. Ives?"

I shook my head in dismay.

"My poor girl," I murmured.

"But I could tell Mummie," she went on excitedly. "I could tell her and Daddy. That was just as good, wasn't it?" She laughed bitterly. "Nobody could care for me enough to put up with Mummie and Daddy. Could they? I ask you, *could* they?"

There was a bench overlooking the sea, and I led her to it and made her sit down. I sat beside her while she gave herself over to her sobs, deep, shaking sobs that seemed as though they would tear her apart. I had never witnessed so complete a disintegration in a human being before. It was beyond sympathy. I waited until her sobs had subsided, holding her hand, and when it was over and she had dried her eyes we walked on to the club. There was no other place to go.

5

All during that fall, after my return to New York, I found myself worrying about Isabella. It had not even occurred to me for a moment, prior to my meeting with her on the cliff walk, that I had not behaved in every respect as a loving parent should have. It had seemed so obvious that the Duntons were undesirable and that Alex was too young to look after himself. What could a girl brought up as she offer to counterbalance such arguments? I still felt that I had done right; I still did not wish her for a daughter-in-law, but my peace of mind was troubled now by the persistent picture of the suffering locked up behind those nervous, flitting eyes. The more I thought about it, the more I felt the desire to do something in compensation, something, that is, short of surrendering Alex to the Dunton fold. I had never told Rosa about the scene on the cliff walk, but I mentioned Isabella's family to her from time to time.

"I wonder what they do in winter," I said once. "Do people like that have an existence in winter?"

Rosa, however, since the day that Alice Dunton had left the house in disgust, had ceased to take their part. She looked for the best in people, but her loyalty to me, as mine to her, was complete, and Alice Dunton, she felt, had insulted me.

"I'm sure I have no idea," she said dispassionately. "Perhaps they go to Florida. The people there, I'm told, are even richer than you."

"Does Isabella go?"

"I imagine."

But I wanted to talk about Isabella. I would have welcomed a return of the warm sentiment in Rosa which I had so deplored in Anchor Harbor.

"Do you suppose she pines for Alex?" I asked.

Rosa shrugged her shoulders.

"She won't break her heart," she answered. "Her mother will find her a more compliant father-in-law."

Alex's attitude also gave me some concern. He had gone back to Harvard, but he came to New York more frequently than he had the year before. It was not, Rosa assured me, to see Isabella. He took other girls out and spent a lot of money in night clubs. He bought a new car and, more gradually, a new wardrobe. In fact, he showed definite signs of becoming sophisticated. He never mentioned Isabella, but, obviously, the topic was an impossible one. And I worried about the fact that he, like Rosa, was doing her an injustice.

My preoccupation came out one day when Rosa asked me, during the Christmas holidays, if she could give a dinner dance at my apartment for a girl whose parents, like so many of Rosa's friends, had suffered too many reversals to be able to give parties themselves. Rosa was always giving such dinners; it was the only way, except for donations to charities, that I could ever spend my money to her gratification.

"I wonder," I said, a bit self-consciously, "if it wouldn't be nice to ask Isabella Dunton. It seems rather artificial *never* to see her. Don't you think? After all, poor girl, I owe her something. She didn't marry Alex."

Rosa looked troubled. She could never bear to have a veto attributed to herself.

"Well, maybe," she said doubtfully. "After all, it's going to be a large party. But won't she be in Florida?"

She was not, it turned out, in Florida, and she accepted, as Duntons always did, with the greatest of pleasure. I told Alex on his next weekend in New York, but he simply looked at me, with a rather funny smile, and shrugged his shoulders.

I usually enjoyed Rosa's parties for the young, but I was not at my ease that night as I stood by the big fireplace in the parlor with Alex as the guests arrived. It was not particularly a group of his friends, and he seemed rather to be showing off his aloofness by standing aside with his father and displaying what he appeared to consider the smart informality of his velvet smoking jacket. I was watching the door too nervously to pay attention to what he was saying, but finally, as I had turned to throw my cigarette in the fire, I heard him murmur:

"Look, Dad."

I turned back to see her coming towards us, in bright red with her hair as carefully done as ever, smiling in the uncertain way of the shortsighted. She paused for a moment, squinting, and then came quickly forward to put her hand in mine.

"Good evening, Mr. Ives," she said in her usual tone. "It was so good of you and Miss Ives to ask me. It's such a pleasure to see one's summer friends in the winter. Such a rare treat." She looked at me with bright, expectant eyes while I said nothing. I could barely smile. "And if it isn't Alex!" she exclaimed, turning to him as if she were performing a part in a school play. "Well, well. Long time no see." She laughed, nervously, appallingly. "We're certainly the picture of health, aren't we? Canada did us good, I guess?"

Alex smiled sheepishly. I could see that he was avoiding my eyes.

"You're looking pretty well, yourself, Isabella," he said.

"Oh, me?" She turned to me and laughed again. "I'm always in the pink. Aren't I, Miss Ives?" she asked Rosa who came up to us at this moment. "I was telling Mr. Ives and Alex that I'm always in the pink. I am, am I not?"

Rosa's smile to Alex and myself excluded Isabella.

"It seems an odd color," she said, "for a Dunton to boast of."

I felt in their laugh, Rosa's and Alex's, the full impact of their mutual desire to make up for any unfairness that they might have shown to me during the summer. It was there, I knew, that appeal, and from those I loved best in the world, to have things, without further ado or explanations, as they had always been. As I looked back into Isabella's frightened eyes and frightened smile I felt an odd small reawakening of my bitterness against her that she should once more stand between me and my son.

"I think dinner has been announced," I said, and Alex and I stood alone together by the fireplace as we watched the ladies slowly following Rosa and Isabella into the dining room. I felt his hand on my arm in a friendly, filial grip.

"How right you were about all that business, Dad," he murmured in my ear. "When I think about what could have been! God, I must have been crazy! If you catch me getting that way again, keep an eye on me, will you, old man?"

I smiled, instinctively, and put my arm around his shoulder, as I always did when Alex confided in me, but as we walked on into the dining room after the other men I felt the bitterness of knowing that he would not be needing me again.

MAUD

*Home is where one starts from. As we grow older
The world becomes stranger, the pattern more complicated
Of dead and living.*
—T. S. Eliot, *Four Quartets*

MAUD

A<small>LL</small> M<small>AUD</small>'<small>S</small> <small>LIFE</small> it had seemed to her that she was like a dried-up spring at the edge of which her devoted relatives and friends used to gather hopefully in the expectation that at least a faint trickle might appear. Their own natures, it seemed, were rich with the bubbling fluid of hearty emotion, and their very repleteness made her own sterility the more remarkable. She gazed back at them; she tried to feel what they felt, tried to respond to their yearning glances. But what was the use? It had been her lot to live alone, surrounded by smiles and love, by sports and games and homely affection, through cold winters with warm fires and long, bright, boisterous summers. To Maud, the Spreddons seemed to be always circling, hand in hand, the bonfire of their own joy in life. Could they mean it? she would sometimes ask herself. Yet in sober truth they seemed to be what they appeared. Daddy, large and hearty, was always spoken of as one of the best lawyers downtown and was certainly a rich man, too, despite his eternal jangle about being the average father of an average American family. Mummie, stout and handsome, bustled with good works, and the morning mail was always filled with invitations to accept the chairmanship of worthy drives. Brother Fred was captain of his school football team; brother Sam was head of his class; Grandpapa was the good old judge whom all had revered, and beautiful Granny one of the "last" of the great ladies — there was no end to it.

But why did they always think that they had to draw *her* in, make *her* part of it? Why did they all turn to her on those ghastly Christmas Eves, when they gathered around the piano to bray out their carols, and cry: "Maud, sing this," and "Maud, isn't it lovely?" And why, when, with the devil in her soul, she raised her uncertain voice to sing the page's part in "Good King Wenceslaus," did they say: "That was *really* nice, Maud. You do like Christmas, don't you, after all?" It was the "after all" that gave them away. They smelled her out, spotted her for what she was, a rank intruder in their midst; but at the same time, with inexhaustible generosity, they held open the gate and continued to shout their welcome.

"Damn you! Damn all of you!"

There. She had said it, and she had said it, too, on Christmas Eve, one week after her thirteenth birthday. Not as long as she lived would she forget the shocked hush that fell over the family group, the stern amazement of her father, the delighted animosity of the boys. It was out at last.

"Maud!" her father exclaimed. "Where did you ever pick up language like that?"

"From Nannie," she answered.

"From Nannie!"

"Darling!" cried her mother, enveloping her with arms of steel. "Darling child, what's wrong? Aren't you happy? Tell Mummie, dearest."

"Maud's wicked," said brother Sam.

"Shut up, Sam," his father snapped.

Pressed to the lacy warmness of her mother's bosom, Maud felt welling up within herself the almost irresistible tide of surrender, but when she closed her eyes and clenched her fists, her own little granite integrity was able, after all, to have its day. She tore herself out of her mother's arms.

"I hate you all!" she screamed.

This time there was no sternness or hostility in the eyes around her. There was only concern, deep concern.

"I'll take her up to her room," she heard her mother tell her father. "You stay here. Tell Nannie, if she hasn't already gone out, to stay."

Her mother took her upstairs and tried to reason with her. She talked to her very gently and told her how much they all loved her and how much they would do for her, and didn't she love them back just a little, tiny, tiny bit? Didn't she really, darling? But Maud was able to shake her head. It was difficult; it cost her much. Everything that was in her was yearning to have things the way they had always been, to be approved and smiled at, even critically, but she knew how base it would be to give in to the yearning, even if everything that stood for resistance was baser yet. She was a bad girl, a very bad one, but to go back now, to retrace her steps, after the passionately desired and unbelievably actual stand of defiance, to merge once more with that foolish sea of smiles and kisses, to lose forever her own little ego in the consuming fire of family admiration — no, this she would not do.

Alone in the dark she flung herself upon her pillow and made it damp with her tears, tears that for the first time in her life came from her own causing. Why she was taking this dark and lonely course, why she should have to persist in setting herself apart from all that was warm and beckoning, she could only wonder, but that she *was* doing it and would continue to do it and would live by it was now her dusky faith. "I will. I will. I *will!*" she repeated over and over, until she had worked herself into a sort of frenzy and was banging her head against the bedpost. Then the door opened, swiftly, as though they had been standing just outside, and her mother and father and Nannie came in and looked at her in dismay.

2

Mrs. Spreddon had certainly no idea what had possessed her daughter. She was not without intelligence or sympathy, and responsibility sat easily with the furs on her ample shoulders, but there was little imagination and no humor in her make-up, and she could not comprehend any refusal of others to participate in that portion of the good of the universe which had been so generously allotted to herself. The disappointments that resulted from a failure to achieve an aim, any aim, were well within her comprehension, and when her son Sammy had failed to be elected head monitor of his school she and Mr. Spreddon had journeyed to New England to be at his side; but misery without a cause or misery with bitterness was to her unfathomable. She discussed it with her husband's sister, Mrs. Lane, who was in New York on a visit from Paris. Lila Lane was pretty, diminutive, and very chatty. She laughed at herself and the world and pretended to worship politics when she really worshiped good food. She dressed perfectly, always in black, with many small diamonds.

"It isn't as if the child didn't have everything she wanted," Mrs. Spreddon pointed out. "All she has to do is ask, and she gets it. Within limits, of course. I'm not one to spoil a child. What could it be that she's dissatisfied with?"

Mrs. Lane, taking in the detail of her sister-in-law's redecorated parlor, heavily and perfectly Georgian, all gleaming mahogany and bright new needlework, reflected that Maud might, after all, have something to be dissatisfied with.

"Is she ever alone?" she asked.

"Why should she be alone?" Mrs. Spreddon demanded. "She's far too shy as it is. She hates playing with other children. She hasn't a single friend at school that I know of."

"Neither did I. At that age."

Mrs. Spreddon was not surprised to hear this, but then she had no intention of having her Maud grow up like Lila and perhaps live in Paris and buy a Monet every fifth year with the money that she saved by not having children.

"But Maud doesn't like *anybody*," she protested. "Not even me."

"Why should she?"

"Oh, Lila. You've been abroad too long. Whoever heard of a child not liking her own family when they've been good to her?"

"I have. Just now."

Mrs. Spreddon frowned at her. "You seem to think it's my fault," she said.

"It isn't anyone's fault, Mary," Mrs. Lane assured her. "Maud didn't choose you for a mother. There's no reason she should like you."

"And what should I do about it?"

Mrs. Lane shrugged her shoulders. "Is there anything to be done?" she asked. "Isn't the milk pretty well spilled by now?"

"That's all very well for you to say," Mrs. Spreddon retorted. "But a parent can't take that point of view. A parent has to believe."

"I don't mean that she's hopeless," Mrs. Lane said quickly. "I just mean that she's different. There's nothing so terrible about that, Mary. Maud's more like her grandfather."

"The Judge? But he was such an old dear, Lila!"

Mrs. Lane placed a cigarette carefully in her ivory holder and held it for several seconds before lighting it. She hated disputes, but the refusal of her sister-in-law to face any facts at all in the personalities around her other than the cheerful ones that she attributed to them, a refusal that Mrs. Lane felt to be indigenous to the stratum of American life that she had abandoned for Paris, irritated her almost beyond endurance.

"My father was not an 'old dear,' Mary," she said in a rather metallic tone. "He was a very intellectual and a very strange man. He was never really happy until they made him a judge, and he could sit on a bench, huddled in his black robes, and look out at the world."

"You have such a peculiar way of looking at things, Lila," Mrs. Spreddon retorted. "Judge Spreddon was a great man. Certainly, I never knew a man who was more loved."

Mrs. Lane inhaled deeply. "Maybe Maud's daughters-in-law will say the same about her."

"Maybe they will," Mrs. Spreddon agreed. "If she ever has any."

Mr. Spreddon worried even more than his wife, but he knew better than to expose himself to the chilly wind of his sister's skepticism. When he sought consolation it was in the sympathetic male atmosphere of his downtown world where he could always be sure of a friendly indifference and an easy optimism to reassure his troubled mind. Mr. Spreddon at fifty-five showed no outward symptoms of any inner insecurity. He was a big man of magnificent health, with gray hair and red cheeks, who had succeeded to his father's position in the great law firm that bore his name. Not that this had been an easy or automatic step, or that it could have been accomplished without the distinct ability that Mr. Spreddon possessed. He was an affable and practical-minded man whose advice was listened to with respect at directors' meetings and by the widows and daughters of the rich. But it was true, nevertheless, that beneath the joviality of his exterior he carried a variegated sense of guilt: guilt at having succeeded a father whose name was so famous in the annals of law, guilt at having leisure in an office where people worked so hard, guilt at being a successful lawyer without having ever argued a case, guilt at suspecting that the sound practical judgment for which he was reputed was, in the last analysis, nothing but a miscellany of easy generalities. It may have been for this reason that he took so paternal an interest in the younger lawyers in his office, particularly in Halsted Nicholas, the prodigy from Yonkers who had started as an office boy and had been Judge Spreddon's law clerk when the old man died.

"I tell you she's all right, Bill," Halsted said with his usual familiarity when Mr. Spreddon came into the little office where he was working surrounded by piles of photostatic exhibits, both feet on his desk. "You ought to be proud of her. She's got spunk, that girl."

"You'll admit it's an unusual way to show it."

"All the better. Originality should be watered." Halsted swung around in his chair to face the large ascetic features of the late Judge Spreddon in the photograph over his bookcase. "The old boy would have approved," he added irreverently. "He always said it was hate that made the world go round."

Mr. Spreddon never quite knew what to make of Halsted's remarks. "But I don't want her to be abnormal," he said. "If she goes on hating everybody, how is she ever going to grow up and get married?"

"Oh, she'll get married," Halsted said.

"Well, sure. If she changes."

"Even if she doesn't."

Mr. Spreddon stared. "Now, what makes you say that?" he demanded.

"Take me. I'll marry her."

Mr. Spreddon laughed. "You'll have to wait quite a bit, my boy," he said. "She's only thirteen."

3

Mr. and Mrs. Spreddon were not content with the passive view recommended by Mrs. Lane and Halsted Nicholas. Conscientious and loving parents as they were, they recognized that what ailed Maud was certainly something beyond their own limited control, and they turned, accordingly, in full humility and with open purses, to the psychiatrist, the special school, the tutor, the traveling companion. In fact, the whole paraphernalia of our modern effort to adjust the unadjusted was brought to bear on their sulking daughter. Nobody ever spoke to Maud now except with predetermined cheerfulness. She was taken out of the home that she had so disliked and sent to different schools in different climates, always in the smiling company of a competent woman beneath whose comfortable old-maid exterior was hidden a wealth of expensive psychological experience, and whose well-paid task it was to see if somehow it was not possible to pry open poor tightened Maud and permit the entry of at least a trickle of spontaneity. Maud spent a year in Switzerland under the care of one of the greatest of doctors, who regularly devoted one morning a week to walking with her in a Geneva park; she spent a year in Austria under equally famous auspices, and she passed two long years in Arizona in a small private school where she rode and walked with her companion and enjoyed something like peace. During visits home she was treated with a very special consideration, and her brothers were instructed always to be nice to her.

Maud saw through it all, however, from the very first and resented it with a continuing intensity. It was the old battle that had always raged between herself and her family; of this she never lost sight, and to give in because the struggle had changed its form would have been to lose the only fierce little logic that existed in her drab life. To this she clung with the dedication of a vestal virgin, wrapping herself each year more securely in the coating of her own isolation. Maud learned a certain adjustment to life, but she lost none of the bitterness of her conflict in the process. At nineteen she still faced the world with defiance in her eyes.

When she returned from the last of her many schools and

excursions and came home to live with her family in New York, it was just six years from the ugly Christmas Eve of her original explosion. She had grown up into a girl whose appearance might have been handsome had one not been vaguely conscious of a presence somehow behind her holding her back — a person, so to speak, to whom one could imagine her referring questions over her shoulder and whose answer always seemed to be no. She had lovely, long, dark hair which she wore, smooth and uncurled, almost to her shoulders; she was very thin, and her skin was a clear white. Her eyes, large and brown, had a steady, uncompromising stare. She gave all the appearance of great shyness and reserve, for she hardly spoke at all, but the settled quality of her stare made it evident that any reluctance on her part to join in general conversation did not have its origin in timidity. Maud had established her individuality and her prejudices, and it was felt that this time she had come home to stay. Her parents still made spasmodic efforts to induce her to do this thing or that, but essentially her objectives had been attained. Nobody expected anything of her. Nobody was surprised when she did not kiss them.

She adopted for herself an unvarying routine. Three days a week she worked at a hospital; she rode in Central Park; she read and played the piano and occasionally visited the Metropolitan. Mrs. Spreddon continued the busy whirl of her life and reserved teatime every evening as her time for Maud. What more could she do? It was difficult to work up any sort of social life for a daughter so reluctant, but she did make occasional efforts and managed once in a while to assemble a stiff little dinner for Maud where the guests would be taken on, immediately upon rising from table, to the best musical comedy of the season, the only bait that could have lured them there. Maud endured it without comment. She was willing to pay an occasional tax for her otherwise unruffled existence.

At one of these dinners, she found Halsted Nicholas seated on her right. She remembered him from earlier days when he had spent summers with them as her brothers' tutor, and her memories of that summer were pleasanter than most. He was, of course, no longer a boy, being close to thirty-five, and a junior partner now of her father's; but his face had lost none of the sensitivity and charm, none of the uncompromising youth that she dimly remembered. He seemed an odd combination of ease and tension; one could tell that his reserve and even his air of gentle timidity were the product of manners; for when he spoke, it was with a certain roughness that indicated assurance. This was reinforced by the intent stare with which he fastened his very round and dark eyes on his plate and the manner in which his black eyebrows seemed to ripple with his thick black hair. She would have liked to talk to him, but that, of course, was not her way, and she watched him carefully as he crumbled his roll on the thick white tablecloth.

"You've certainly been taking your own sweet time to grow up, Maud," he said in a familiar tone, breaking a cracker into several pieces and dropping them into his soup as Maud had been taught never to do. "This makes it six years that I've been waiting for you."

"Six years?" she repeated in surprise.

He nodded, looking at her gravely. "Six years," he said. "Ever since that wonderful Christmas Eve when you told the assembled Spreddon family to put on their best bib and tucker and jump in the lake."

Maud turned pale. Even the heavy silver service on the long table seemed to be jumping back and forth. She put down her spoon. "So you know that," she said in a low voice. "They talk about it. They tell strangers."

He laughed his loud, easy laugh. "I'm hardly a stranger, Maud," he said. "I've been working as a lawyer in your father's office for twelve years and before that I was there as an office boy. And you're wrong about their telling people, too. They didn't have to tell me. I was there."

She gasped. "You couldn't have been," she protested. "I remember it so well." She paused. "But why are you saying this, anyway? What's the point?"

Again he laughed. "You don't believe me," he said. "But it's so simple. It was Christmas Eve and I was all alone in town, and your old man, who, in case you don't know it, is one prince of a guy, took pity on me and asked me up. I told him I'd come in a Santa Claus get-up and surprise you kids. Anyway I was right in here, in this very dining room, sticking my beard on and peering through the crack in those double doors to watch for my cue from your father when — bingo! — you pulled that scene. Right there before my eyes and ears! Oh, Maud! You were terrific!"

Even with his eyes, his sure but friendly eyes, upon her as he said all this, it was as if it were Christmas again, Christmas with every stocking crammed and to be emptied, item by item, before the shining and expectant parental faces. Maud felt her stomach muscles suddenly tighten in anguished humiliation. She put her napkin on the table and looked desperately about her.

"Now Maud," he said, putting his firm hand on hers. "Take it easy."

"Leave me alone," she said in a rough whisper. "Leave me be."

"You're not going to be angry with me?" he protested. "After all these years? All these years that I've been waiting for the little girl with the big temper to grow up? Maud, how unkind."

She gave him a swift look. "I've been back home and grown up for several months," she pointed out ungraciously. "If you know Father so well, you must have known that. And this is the first time you've been to the house."

He shrugged his shoulders. "Lawyers are busy men, Maud," he said. "We can't get off every night. Besides, I'm shy."

She was not to be appeased so lightly. "You didn't come to see me, anyway," she retorted. "You came because Daddy begged you to." She smiled sourly. "He probably went down on his knees."

"Nothing of the sort," he said coolly. "If you must know, I came because I heard we were going to *Roll Out the Barrel.*"

Maud stared at him for a second and then burst out laughing. "Then you're in for a sad disappointment, Mr. Nicholas," she said, "because Daddy couldn't get seats. We're going to *Doubles or Quits.* I do hope you haven't seen it."

He covered his face with his napkin. "But I have," he groaned. "Twice!"

Maud, of course, did not know it, but Halsted Nicholas was the partner who, more than any other, held the clients of Spreddon & Spreddon. Mr. Spreddon increasingly accepted positions of public trust; he was now president of a museum, a hospital, and a zoo, all the biggest of their kind; he represented to his partners that this sort of thing, although unremunerative and time-consuming, "paid dividends in the long run." If anyone grumbled, it was not Halsted, whose industry was prodigious. What drove him so hard nobody knew. He never showed ambition of the ordinary sort, as, for example, wanting his name at the top of the firm letterhead or asking for paneling in his office. He felt, it was true, the deepest gratitude to Mr. Spreddon and to his late father, the Judge, who had seen promise in him and who had sent him to college and law school, but this he had already repaid a hundredfold. He loved the law, it was true, but he was already one of the ablest trial lawyers in the city and could certainly have held his position without quite so liberal an expenditure of energy. No, if Halsted was industrious it was probably by habit. He may have lacked the courage to stop and look into himself. He was a man who had met and undertaken many responsibilities; he had supported his friends with advice and his parents with money; he was considered to be — and, indeed, he was — an admirable character, unspoiled even by a Manhattan success; but whatever part of himself he revealed, it was a public part. His private self was unshared.

He left the theater that night after the second act to go down to his office and work on a brief, but the following Sunday he called at the Spreddons' and took Maud for a walk around the reservoir. A week later he invited her to come to Wall Street to dine with him, on the excuse that he had to work after dinner and could not get uptown, and after she had done this, which he said no other girl would have done, even for Clark Gable, he became a steady caller at the Spreddons'. Maud found herself in the unprecedented situation of having a beau.

He was not a very ceremonious beau; he never sent her flowers or whispered silly things in her ear, and not infrequently, at the very last moment, when they had planned an evening at the theater or the opera, he would call up to say that he couldn't get away from the office. Maud, however, saw nothing unusual in this. What mattered to her was that he expected so little. He never pried into her past or demanded her agreement or enthusiasm over anything; he never asked her to meet groups of his friends or to go to crowded night clubs. He never, furthermore, offered the slightest criticism of her way of living or made suggestions as to how she might enlarge its scope. He took her entirely for granted and would, without any semblance of apology, talk for an entire evening about his own life and struggles and the wonderful things that he had done in court. She was a slow talker, and he a fast one; it was easier for both if he held forth alone on the subjects closest to his heart. In short, she became accustomed to him; he fitted in with her riding and her hospital work. She had been worried at first, particularly in view of his initial revelation, never thereafter alluded to, of what he had once witnessed, but soon afterwards she had been reassured. It was all right. He would let her be.

4

Mr. and Mrs. Spreddon, in the meantime, were holding their breath. They had almost given up the idea that Maud would ever attract any man, much less a bachelor as eligible as Halsted. It was decided, after several conferences, that what nature had so miraculously started, nature might finish herself, and they resolved not to interfere. This, unfortunately, they were not able to do without a certain ostentation, and Maud became aware of an increasing failure on the part of her family to ask their usual questions about what she had done the night before and what meals she expected to eat at home the following day. If she referred to Halsted, her comment received the briefest of nods or answers. Nobody observing the fleeting references with which his name was dismissed at the Spreddon board would ever have guessed that the parental hearts were throbbing at the mere possibility of his assimilation into the family.

Maud, however, was not to be fooled. The suppressed wink behind the family conspiracy of silence was almost lewd to her, and it brought up poignantly the possibility that Halsted might be thinking of their friendship in the same way. It was true that he had said nothing to her that could even remotely be construed as sentimental, but it was also true, she realized ruefully, that she knew very little of such things, and the effusive, confiding creature to whom her brother Sammy was engaged, who frequently made her uncomfortable by trying to drag her into long intimate chats "just between us girls," had told her that when men took one out it was never for one's society alone and that this went for a certain "you know who" in the legal world as well as anyone else, even if he *was* somewhat older. Maud seemed to feel her breath stop at this new complication in a life settled after so many disturbances. Was this not the very thing that she had always feared, carried to its worst extreme? Was this not the emotion that was reputedly the most demanding, the most exacting of all the impulses of the heart? She had a vision of bridesmaids reaching for a thrown bouquet and faces looking up at her to where she was standing in unbecoming satin on a high stair — faces covered with frozen smiles and eyes, seas of eyes, black and staring and united to convey the same sharp, hysterical message: Aren't you happy? Aren't you in love? Now, then, didn't we *tell* you?

The next time Halsted called up she told him flatly that she had a headache. He took it very casually and called again about a week later. She didn't dare use the same excuse, and she couldn't think of another, so she met him for dinner at a French restaurant. She nibbled nervously on an olive while he drank his second cocktail in silence, watching her.

"Somebody's gone and frightened you again," he said with just an edge of roughness in his voice. "What's it all about? Why did you fake that headache last week?"

She looked at him miserably. "I didn't."

"Why did you have it then?"

"Oh." She raised her hand to her brow and rubbed it in a preoccupied manner. "Well, I guess I thought we were going out too much together."

"Too much for what?"

"Oh. You know."

"Were you afraid of being compromised?" he asked sarcastically.

"Please, Halsted," she begged him. "You know how people are. I like going out with you. I love it, really. But the family all wink and nod. They can't believe that you and I are just good friends. They'll be expecting you — well, to say something."

He burst out laughing. "And you're afraid I won't. I see."

She shook her head. "No," she said gravely, looking down at her plate; "I'm afraid you will."

He stopped laughing and looked at her intently. Then he gave a low whistle. "Well!" he exclaimed. "So that's how it is. And this is the girl whose father used to say that she had no self-confidence! Well, I'll be damned!"

Maud blushed. "You mustn't think I'm conceited," she

said with embarrassment. "It's not that at all. I just don't understand these things. Really." She looked at him, imploring him not to take it amiss.

"Look, Maud," he said more gently, taking her hand in his. "Can't you trust me? I know all about it. Honest."

"All about what, Halsted?"

"What you're afraid of. Listen to me, my sweet. Nobody's going to make you do any falling in love. Nobody could. Yet. Do you get that? It's just possible that I may ask you to marry me. We'll see. But in any case I'm not going to ask you how you feel about me. That's your affair. Is that clear?"

She looked into his large and serious eyes and felt her fears subside. It was true that he was completely honest. He did not even tighten his grip on her hand.

"But why should you ever want to marry me?" she asked. "Nobody likes me."

"Give them time, darling," he said, smiling as she withdrew her hand from his. "They will. You want to know why I should be thinking about marrying you? Very well. That's a fair question. I'm thirty-four. There's one reason. It's high time, you'll admit. And I'm not so attractive that I can pick anyone I want. I have to take what I can get." And again he laughed.

"But don't you feel you could do better than me?" she asked seriously. "I'm really a terrible poke. Besides, Sammy says you make all sorts of money. That should help."

He shrugged his shoulders. "Oh, I haven't quite given up," he said cheerfully. "Don't get your hopes too high."

This time she smiled too. "You mean I'm only a last resort?"

Again he put his hand on hers. "Not quite. There's another point in your favor, Maud," he said. "If you must know."

"And what's that?"

He looked at her for a moment, and she suddenly knew that they were going to be very serious indeed.

"I wasn't going to mention it," he continued, "but I might as well now. I'm in love with you, Maud."

She could only shake her head several times in quick succession as if to stop him. "Why?" she asked. "What do you see in me?"

He shrugged his shoulders. "Who knows?" he said. "Call it the desire to protect. Or the mother instinct. Or just plain middle-aged folly. It might be anything. But, Maud, you wouldn't believe it. I can even catch myself thinking about you in court."

They looked at each other gravely for several seconds.

"Well, I suppose that does it," she said, smiling. "I'll have to marry you now."

He raised his hand. "Wait a moment!" he warned her. "First you've got to be asked. And after that you've got to think it over. For several days. I want no fly-by-night answer."

Halsted did things in his own way, and he adhered strictly to a program laid down by himself. Three days later she received a telegram from Chicago, where he had gone on business, saying: "This is the formal offer. Think it over. See you Friday."

Maud did think it over. In fact, she had thought of nothing else since it had first occurred to her that he might do this. She examined the state of her heart and asked herself if her feeling for Halsted could, even by the watered-down standards of her own emotions, be called love, and she decided that it probably could not. She then tried to analyze what it was that she did feel for him; it was certainly the friendliest feeling that she had ever experienced for another human being. She asked herself if she was not lucky indeed — miraculously lucky — to have run into the one man, probably in the whole country, who wanted her as she was. She visualized the joy of sudden and final liberation from her family. And then too, undeniably, she felt stirring within her the first faint manifestations of a new little pride in her own self that she could pull this off, that she could mean so much to a man like Halsted, a good man, an able man, a man whom people looked up to; she thought of Sammy and his silly little fiancée, and of her worried parents and their hopelessness about her; she pictured the amazement of the family friends. She stood before her mirror and pushed the hair out of her face and tossed her head in sudden resolution.

When Halsted called for her on Friday night she was waiting for him in the front hall with her hat and coat on. She was so nervous that she didn't even allow him to speak.

"Halsted," she said, and the words tumbled out. "I've decided. I will. Definitely."

He walked slowly across the front hall to the bottom step of the circular stairway where she was standing and took both her hands in his. For a long tense moment he looked at her.

"Darling," he said and then laughed. "I thought you'd never make up your mind!"

5

Halsted's courtship occurred during the winter of the first year of the war in Europe. It was the period of the "phony war," which, however much it may have bothered Halsted, was of little concern to Maud. For her the fall of France had as its immediate consequence the precipitous return of her father's sister, Lila Lane, from Paris. Aunt Lila took up her residence, as was to be expected, with her brother, and family meals came to be held in respectful silence while she expounded in her own graphic fashion on her hasty departure from Paris, the forced abandonment of her Renault in a roadside ditch, and her successful arrival, half-starved but with all her diamonds, in an unfamiliar and unfriendly Madrid.

It was not an easy time for her unenthusiastic sister-in law. Mrs. Spreddon was hardly able, in the untroubled safety of her New York home, to debunk these experiences, simply because they had happened to Lila. She was obliged to give lip service to the family idea that Lila for once in her life had come up against the fundamentals, things that in the Spreddon mind loomed as vast round bollards on the long dock of a routine existence. Maud's mother could only bide her time, provoking as it might be, and stop for a bit to listen to Lila's tales.

Maud, as might have been expected, did not think as her mother did. Feeling as she had always felt about the restricted atmosphere of her family life, she thought of this aunt in Paris, with perfect clothes and no children, as the desired antithesis of the boisterous and the vulgar. The vision of Lila's garden and the marble fountain surrounded by the bit of lawn, so closely cut and brightly green, which Maud had seen as a child from the grilled balcony of the exquisite house on the rue de Varenne had always lingered in her mind as the essence of everything that was cool and formal and wonderfully independent. It was no wonder that she hovered expectantly before the exotic gateway of her aunt's existence. And Lila, in her turn, appreciating this silent devotion, particularly from a Spreddon, and having always regarded Maud's troubles as the result of a life spent in the limelight of her sister-in-law's exuberant wealth and bad taste, turned as much of her attention as she could spare from hats to Maud and her singular love life. There were long morning conferences in Lila's littered room over a very little toast and a great deal of coffee.

She had, of course, insisted on meeting Halsted; they lunched, the three of them, one Saturday noon at a small French midtown restaurant, and, as poor Maud could clearly see, it had not gone well. Lila had spent the meal telling Halsted the well-known story, already published in a women's magazine, of her arduous escape from the Germans. Halsted, taciturn and obviously unimpressed, had said almost nothing. But it was later, when Maud was having tea and an early cocktail alone with her aunt, that the important conversation occurred.

"I hope you like him, Aunt Lila," Maud said timidly. "Mother and Daddy do, but, of course, they would. He's a wonderful lawyer. But you've lived abroad and know about people."

Lila Lane inserted a cigarette in her holder and surveyed her niece's almost expressionless face. She prided herself on being the one member of the family who had a kindred sense of the deep antipathies that had gone into Maud's make-up, and she saw her niece's solution along the lines of her own life. "I certainly like him, my dear," she said in a definite tone. "He's obviously a very fine and a very intelligent man. In fact, I shouldn't be surprised if I'm not a little afraid of him. He's *un peu farouche,* if you see what I mean. But attractive. Undeniably."

"Oh, he is, isn't he?"

Lila hesitated a moment before trying a stroke of sophistication. To clear the air. "All in all, my dear," she said with a smile, "an excellent first marriage."

"Oh, Aunt Lila!" Maud's eyes were filled with protest. "What do you mean?"

Her aunt reached over and patted her hand. "Now there, dear, don't get excited. You must let the old Paris aunt have her little joke. You see, Maud, as you say, I've lived abroad. A long time. I've been used to people who are, well — to say the least — stimulating. Your young man, who isn't, by the way, so frightfully young, is more of your father's world. Of course it was my father's world, too. But it's certainly a world that I myself could never be happy in. And I hope you'll forgive me for saying so, my dear, but I have my doubts if you ever could, either. It's a dull world, Maud."

"But I'm dull, Aunt Lila!" Maud protested. "I'm a thousand times duller than Halsted!"

Her aunt looked suddenly stern. "Don't let me ever hear you say that again!" she exclaimed. She got up and took Maud to the mirror over the mantel. "Take a good look at yourself! Your skin. Those eyes. They're good, my dear. Very good." She took Maud's long hair and arranged it in a sort of pompadour over her forehead. "You haven't tried, Maud. That's all. You could be beautiful."

Maud stared at her reflection with momentary fascination, and then turned abruptly away. She shrugged her shoulders. "I'd still be dull."

"Beautiful women are never dull," Lila said, sitting down again at the tea table. "But now I'm sounding like a rather bad Oscar Wilde. Tell me, my dear. In all seriousness. Are you in love with this wonderful lawyer?"

Maud's face was filled with dismay as she stared down at the floor. Neither her mother nor Halsted had presumed to ask her such a question, but there was no escaping it. Now she had to hear it from the lips of Aunt Lila, who spoke, she felt, with an authority that could not be resented. Whatever love may have been to the Spreddons — and Maud, when she thought of it, had a sense of something thick and stifling like a blanket — to Aunt Lila it was a free and glorious emotion that knew not restraint and graced those whom it touched. She was not sure that Aunt Lila had been one so graced, but she had infinite faith in her aunt's ability to observe. Venus had risen, so to speak, on a shell from the sea and was awaiting her answer.

"I really can't say that I am," she answered at last in a low voice. "The way you use the word, anyway."

"The way *I* use the word, Maud! But there's only one way to use it. Either you are or you aren't."

"Oh, Aunt Lila." Maud's eyes filled with tears.

"Listen to me, Maud." Lila had moved over to the sofa and put her arm around her niece. "You know that I love you dearly. Do you think I'd have asked you such an impertinent question if I hadn't been sure that the answer was no?"

Maud shook her head. "Everyone knows about me," she said despairingly. "What should I do?"

"Do?" Lila queried. "You don't have to *do* anything at all. You certainly don't have to marry Halsted because you're *not* in love with him. Maud, darling, if you only knew how I understood! You think you're always going to be bottled up like a clam and that this is the way to make the best of it. But it's not. You're just beginning to stick your head out and peer around. It's absurd to be snapped up by the first one of your father's partners who comes along! Before you've even had a chance to take your bearings!"

But if Maud accepted her aunt as an expert in love, it did not mean that she accepted her as a judge of her own character. She had no interest in her own future, but a very deep interest in her duty to Halsted. Getting up, she went to her room. She sat there by herself for an hour. Then, for the first time in her life, she went to her mother for advice. Mrs. Spreddon was sitting at her dressing table, getting ready for dinner.

"Mother, I'm going to break my engagement to Halsted," she said abruptly.

Mrs. Spreddon eyed her closely in the glass as she fastened a pearl bracelet on her wrist. "May I ask you why?"

"I'm not in love with him."

Mrs. Spreddon was silent for a moment. Then she nodded. "Let me ask you one thing," she said. "Have you been talking to your aunt?"

"I have. But it's not her fault. She said nothing I didn't know already."

"I see."

There was a pause. Then poor Maud blurted forth her appeal. "Mother, what should I do?"

Mrs. Spreddon stood up, very slowly, and turned around. She faced her daughter with dignity, but her voice was trembling. "I'm sorry, Maud," she said. "I'd give anything in the world to be able to help you. You know how your father and I love Halsted. We think he'd be the perfect husband. But this is your life, my dear. Not mine. If we'd had more of a relationship, you and I, we might have been able to work this thing out. God knows I've tried. But parents can take only so much, Maud, and then they're through. You've always wanted to work things out your own way. I'm afraid that now it's too late for me to butt in."

For a long moment they looked at each other, almost in surprise and a little in fear at the sudden reclarification of the gulf between them.

6

It was dark and cool inside the little restaurant where she was to meet Halsted for lunch. When her eyes were adjusted to it, she saw him sitting at the bar talking to the bartender. She went up and sat on the stool beside him, and he smiled and ordered her a drink. Then she told him, straight away. She did it very clearly and rather coldly; she was sure as she looked into his large hurt eyes that she had been convincing.

"But Maud," he protested in a tone almost of exasperation, "we've been through all this before! You know I don't expect anything of you. We can leave that to the future."

"I don't trust the future," she said. "I want to know more about it first."

"Maud, have you gone crazy?"

"It may well be."

There was a pause.

"How can you talk that way, Maud?" he asked suddenly. "How can you be such a smug little — ? Good God! Maud, have you really never given a damn about me? Even one little damn?"

She looked at him steadily. From way back in her past she felt the stirrings of that almost irresistible tide of surrender, the tide that she had dammed so desperately and so decisively on that long ago Christmas Eve. But once again she was the mistress of her fate. "Not in that way, Halsted," she said.

He turned to his unfinished cocktail. "Well, I'll be damned," he said, almost to himself. "I'll be damned."

"You believe me, Halsted, don't you?"

He turned back to her. "I guess I'll have to, Maud," he said. "Maybe I had you doped out all wrong." He shrugged his shoulders. "Lawyers can be persistent," he continued, "but even they know when the game's really up. You'd better go home, Maud. I'll get you a taxi."

He got up and left her, and she knew, as she stared at her reflection in the mirror across the bar, that she was at last doing penance for what she had done that Christmas Eve.

Halsted disappeared from her life as suddenly as he had come into it. Shortly after the fateful meeting, he came into Mr. Spreddon's office, sat down, and putting one leg as usual over the arm of the chair, asked, "Got another litigator around here, Bill? You'll be needing one."

"Oh, Halsted. You too?"

"Me too. I've decided to take that War Department job, after all. Maybe after I've been around there a few months they'll give me a commission. Just to get rid of me."

"Can't you get a commission now?"

"Eyes."

Mr. Spreddon looked broodingly at the photograph of his daughter which stood on his desk between him and Halsted. His heart was heavy. "You must do what you think best, of course," he said sadly. "We'll make out. I'm not trying to hide the fact that it'll be difficult. You know how we stand. This is your firm, Halsted."

Halsted's face clouded with embarrassment. "Cut it out, will you, Bill!" he protested. "You're the whole business around here, and that's the way it should be."

Mr. Spreddon shook his head. "Just a name, my boy. But I won't embarrass you. There's only one thing I'd like to know. Your going to Washington isn't because of Maud, is it?"

Halsted stood up and sauntered around the big office. "Like everyone else," he said in a rather rough tone, while his back was turned to Mr. Spreddon, "I have my own feelings about this war. And they happen to have nothing under the sun to do with your daughter."

"I'm sorry," Mr. Spreddon said meekly. "I shouldn't have mentioned it. But you know how I feel about that. It was the hope of my life."

Halsted shrugged his shoulders and left the room.

Mrs. Spreddon said nothing to Maud when the engagement was broken. She gave her a kiss and offered to send her on a trip. She was seething, however, against her sister-in-law, who, she felt, had betrayed her hospitality. She determined to break openly with her and debated for two days how most cuttingly to accomplish it. Then she went, without consulting her husband, to her sister-in-law's room.

"I hope, Lila," she said in a voice that trembled slightly, "that it gives you some satisfaction to reflect that in all probability you've ruined whatever slight chances Maud may have had for a normal and happy life."

Lila flushed deeply. "I wouldn't expect you to understand, Mary," she answered in a hurt but lofty tone. "All I can say is that anything I may have said to Maud was with her best interests at heart. We differ too fundamentally to make explanations worth while. Under the circumstances I think it would be best if I moved to the Pierre."

"Under the circumstances, I must agree with you."

And so it ended. Halsted wrote Maud from time to time, amusing, impersonal letters, but he never called at the Spreddons' when he came to New York. Then we entered the war, and he got his commission and was one of the first to be sent overseas. Lila tried to cheer Maud up by giving a cocktail party for her at her hotel, but Maud would not even go. Despite what her aunt had said about beautiful women, she still knew that she was dull.

7

Maud joined the Red Cross shortly after the attack on Pearl Harbor. She worked for two years in New York, after which she was sent to Southampton, England. She worked hard and well, serving coffee to literally thousands of young men. When she looked back over her time in uniform she pictured a sea of faces, young and healthy faces; it seemed to her as if there would never be an end to the pressure of youth and vigor and courage upon the barred doors of her heart. But she never yielded, never opened — and anyway, she sometimes wondered, did it matter? They kept passing her tumultuously, and if she had opened the door, just the tiniest crack, and peered out for a glimpse of the surging throng, would anyone have stopped to look or listen, to reach out a hand to her and cry: "Maud, come on! Can't you see us? We're on our *way!*"

If Maud, however, was uncompromising in her attitude

towards the future, she was learning, nonetheless, a new latitude in the examination of her past. She was perfectly willing, even eager, to entertain the possibility that she had, after all, been in love with Halsted from the beginning and still was, but she was afraid to fall into the oversimplifications of wishful thinking. She still had no referent by which to judge love, and though she realized from time to time that she might be losing herself in the forests of introspection, she was capable, in spite of her doubts, of a fierce single-mindedness. There could be no question of other men. If Halsted had been dead she would still have felt an obligation to resolve the incomprehensible problem of her own determination.

Halsted, however, was far from dead. He was in London, and she actually had his address, though she dared not go to see him. She had not even let him know that she was in England. Their correspondence, in fact, had entirely ceased. Now she could see dimly that life might be offering her that rarest of all things, a second and final chance, and she hardly dared face the fact that, in her usual fashion, she was going to let it pass.

Her brother Sammy's destroyer had put in to Southampton at this time, and she was seeing a good deal of him. They had had little enough to say to each other before the war, but now that they were both three thousand miles from their family, they met in the evening in pubs and exchanged confidences with some of the excitement that is shared by new and congenial friends. They drank gin when they could get it and ale when they couldn't, and discussed their parents and themselves with detachment and impartiality. Sammy and his wife were not getting on, and this lent to his conversation the flavor of a superior disillusionment.

"The trouble with you, Maud," he told her one night, "is that you take everything too seriously. You're always analyzing your own emotions. Hell. The thing to do is to grab fun where you can get it. You ought to write Halsted and tell him you're crazy about him."

She looked skeptically at his blond, undoubting face. "But do you really think I am?" she asked.

He shrugged his shoulders. "I think you want to be," he said. "Which is just as good."

"But is that honest, Sammy?"

He laughed. "Do you want to be an old maid, Maud?" he demanded. "A sour, bitter old maid?"

She shook her head. "Not particularly," she answered.

"Well?"

"But I am what I am, aren't I, Sammy?"

"Sure. And you will be what you will be."

He was essentially indifferent, of course, but it was only the indifference of one adult for another. It filled her nonetheless with a bleak loneliness.

"I'm an idiot, Sammy," she said abruptly. "And I'm an idiot to think anyone cares whether or not I'm an idiot. I'll go to London. I'll be like the rest of you."

"That's better, Maud. Much better."

8

When she got her next leave she actually did go to London. She left her bag at the Red Cross on Grosvenor Square and walked down the street to Army Headquarters. It was some time before she found Halsted's office, and then she was unable to send a message to him because he was in conference. She waited in the main hall for an hour and a half.

"He may not even come out for lunch," the sergeant told her.

"I'll wait," she said, and he smiled.

When Halsted, now a lieutenant colonel, looking thinner and serious, walked through the hall he was with several other officers, and there was a preoccupation about their quick stride that made her suddenly feel small and unwanted. She was shrinking back in her chair when he spotted her and stopped.

"Maud!" he exclaimed in astonishment. "Well, I'll be damned!"

He went up to her, holding out both arms, and there was a funny little smile on his face.

"I just dropped in to see you," she stammered.

"Been waiting long?"

"Oh, no."

"Like to go out on the town tonight?" he asked. "For auld lang syne?" He looked at his watch. "I guess I can make it."

She nodded eagerly.

"You're at the Red Cross?" he said. "I'll pick you up at ten."

And he was gone. During the rest of the afternoon, as she wandered through the great and empty rooms of the Victoria and Albert Museum, she speculated in vain on the significance of his smile. He did not pick her up that night until long after ten, for he was again in conference. They drove in his jeep to an officers' club which had formerly been a private house, and a rather elaborate one, and sat at a table in a corner of the large Tudor front hall near the stairway, under which a bar had been installed. Halsted did not seem at all nervous, as she was, but he looked tired and older. He talked about the general aspects of the war in a rather learned way and drank a good deal, but she was too excited to take in a word that he said. He was speculating on the possibilities of a revolution within Germany when she interrupted him.

"Halsted, aren't you going to ask about *me*? And the family? I'm dying to tell. And to hear all about you. But not about the war. Please."

He smiled, just a bit wearily. "How have you been, my dear?" he asked.

"Well, not so terribly well," she began nervously. "But better now. Oh, much better, Halsted. I'm not the fool I was."

It was perfectly evident that he had caught the full import of her words, for he frowned and looked away from her. "When you say you're not the fool you were, Maud," he said in a distant, even a superior tone, "does it by any chance mean that you've changed your mind about me?"

She felt the chill in his voice and hesitated. She held her breath for a moment. "Yes," she said.

He turned and looked at her fixedly, but she could not read the expression in his eyes. "Then as far as you're concerned," he said, "it's on again?"

"Oh, no, Halsted," she said hastily. "Of course not! What do you take me for? It's not 'on' again. I have no claim on you. I've had my chance. Making a mess of things hardly entitles me to another."

"Oh, 'entitles.'" He shrugged his shoulders, almost in irritation as he repeated her word. "When women say they're not 'entitled' to something, what they usually mean is that any man who's not an utter heel would make sure that they get it."

The tears started to Maud's eyes. It was the tone that he had sometimes used in court, or to people whom he thought little of, like Lila, or to the world. Never to her.

"Halsted," she protested in a low voice. "That's not fair."

He looked down into his glass. "Maybe not."

"And it's not like you to be unfair," she continued. "It isn't as if I were expecting you to fall all over me. I know it would be a miracle if you had any feeling left."

He looked even more sullen at this. "But you still feel sorry for yourself," he retorted.

Maud put her napkin on the table and reached for her cigarettes. "Good night, Colonel," she said crisply. "There's nothing like auld lang syne, is there?"

"Nothing."

She got up. "You needn't worry about taking me back," she said. "I can find my way."

"Oh, sit down," he said roughly, but in a more human tone. "We've got a whole bottle of whiskey here. I don't suppose you expect me to get through it alone?"

"I'm sure," she said with dignity, "that I don't care how you get through it. There must be plenty of other officers with desk jobs in London who can help you out."

He caught her by the arm and pulled her back into her chair. "Desk jobs, hell," he muttered and poured her a drink. "Now drink that and shut up. I wish to hell I did have a desk job. Would you like to know where I was last week?"

"We're warned," she said, "not to encourage officers who drink too much and start revealing military information."

He finished his drink in a gulp and leaned his head on his hands. "Oh, Christ, Maud," he said.

She said nothing.

"I don't know why you had to come back," he continued. "The same prim little girl. Just a bit older, that's all. I'd gotten over you, you know. I mean it, God damn it. And I was enjoying my melancholy. I liked feeling a hero and thinking of the little girl back home who didn't give a rap about me, and wouldn't she be sorry now? Oh, I could spit." He reached again for the bottle and poured himself another drink. "Now I don't know what I feel. I wish like hell, Maud, that I could say it's all the way it was, but I'm damned if I know."

She believed him, believed him absolutely, but there was no humiliation or pain in it. For her the long uncertainty had ended. In her excitement his doubts seemed almost irrelevant.

"You needn't worry about it, Halsted," she said. "It seems so fair."

He looked at her suspiciously. "Fair?" he repeated. "You must be an icebox, Maud. How else could you talk that way?"

"It's just that I don't know how to talk," she said humbly. "You know that."

He smiled at her. "Oh, you can talk, Maud."

"You can make your life very difficult by being complicated," she went on. "I ought to know something about that. You can think you ought to be feeling all sorts of things that you don't. The people around you don't help. I've been through that. I was a fool."

He stared hard at her for a moment, but as if he were concentrating on something else. He opened his mouth as if he were about to say something and then closed it.

"Maud," he said finally, looking down again at the table, "would you marry me? If I were to ask you again?"

She nodded gravely. "I would."

"After all I've said?"

"After all you've said."

There was a pause, an interminable pause. Then he suddenly smiled and put his hand on hers. "Well, nobody would be able to say," he said, "that we were rushing into this thing without having given it thought. And yet, somehow, I feel that's just what we would be doing."

She took out her handkerchief at last and wiped her eyes. "We've tried waiting," she pointed out. "And that didn't work."

He laughed.

"Well, I'm game," he said. "I'm always taking chances with my future in these days. I might as well take a fling with my past." He put his hand suddenly around her shoulder. "Poor little Maud," he said, smiling. "Poor helpless little Maud. This is only the second time you've trapped your victim. But don't worry. You won't be able to get out of it this time."

"The only thing I'm worrying about," she observed, with an eye on the diminished bottle, "is getting you back to your quarters sober."

"I see you're starting right," he agreed more cheerfully. "Well, I asked for it. Or did I?"

How it would have worked out they never were to know, for Halsted was killed two days later when his reconnaissance plane was shot down over Cherbourg. They had met only once in the interval, at lunch, for Halsted had been in conference or flying day and night in preparation for the great invasion of France that took place only a week after his death. Into the blackness of Maud's heart there is no need to penetrate. It was fortunate for her that her work increased in intensity during those days.

A few weeks later her club mobile unit crossed to France, where it operated just below the front. A friend of Halsted's sent her a note that he had placed in an envelope marked "Maud Spreddon, Red Cross" just before he had taken off on his last flight. It was simply a line: "Maud, dearest, never forget. You're all right, and you're going to be all right. With me or without me." She had folded the note and placed it in a locket which she wore around her neck and which she never afterwards reopened. She did not tell her parents or even Sammy that she had seen Halsted again before his death, or what had passed between them. Such a tale would have made her a worthy object of the pity that she had so despised herself for seeking. It was her sorrow, and Halsted would have admired her for facing it alone.

THE FALL OF A SPARROW

> There's a special providence in the fall of a sparrow. If it be now, 'tis not to come; if it be not to come, it will be now; if it be not now, yet it will come: the readiness is all.
>
> —HAMLET

THE FALL OF
A SPARROW

B<small>Y THE FINAL WINTER</small> of the war I had lost my enthusiasm for meeting people at officers' clubs. I preferred to do my serious drinking alone. I had been in the navy too long and at sea too steadily to feel much in common with my old friends from school and college. I had been called to duty more than a year before Pearl Harbor; since then I had served on destroyers on North Atlantic convoy, in the Mediterranean and finally in the Pacific. I had frozen into the routine of war, of short leaves in cold English cities, of long night watches, and, more recently, of beer in the afternoon in Quonsett huts surrounded by the dirty sand of Pacific naval bases. The whole thing had come to have some of the lethargic intrigue of a heavy head cold. I had made up my mind that it would never end and that my youth was being hopelessly wasted, and I had got used to thinking this. I had ceased, more or less, to be dissatisfied, but I had no wish to be reminded of my own inertia.

This, perhaps, explains some of the antagonism that I felt towards Victor Harden. It was certainly not poor Victor's intention to demonstrate any difference between his own sharpened consciousness and my dulled reactions. He was always the soul of consideration. But this very contrast, in any event, is what he succeeded in making me feel when I met him in Ulithi.

I was sitting alone at the officers' club on Mog-Mog Island, drinking beer, when I saw him. I had not seen him since we had been classmates in Chelton School in New Hampshire, ten years before, but he had changed very little. His long brown hair was still parted far to one side and fell in the same neat triangle over his forehead; his large dark eyes and high cheekbones conveyed the same impression of good looks that was still spoiled by his air of nervous irresolution. He was a full lieutenant, and he was sitting with a group of ensigns who, I assumed, came from his ship. I could see that he was being polite, in the same careful way that he had been polite at school, and I smiled to see it. Our friendship at Chelton, I remembered, had been of Victor's seeking; he had attached himself to me and had even made a small dent in the isolation that I preferred. But it had been a long time ago, and I was surprised at the enthusiasm with which he greeted me, leaving his table as soon as he saw me.

"Ted!" he exclaimed. "I can't believe it! What are you doing here? Someone told me you were in England."

He sat down at the table, and I gave him a beer and

explained that I was waiting for a new destroyer that I had been assigned to.

"A tin can!" he exclaimed. "Think of it! What'll you be?" He took in the maple leaf on my crumpled collar. "Exec?"

I nodded.

He seemed impressed. He made me give him a short history of the ships I had been on and the places I had been to. He seemed discouraged at the quantity of them and the contrast that they afforded to his own career.

"Of course, I've been breaking my neck to get sea duty from the beginning," he explained. "But Admiral Lawrence, my boss in Washington, refused to release me. Just refused, point-blank. Then, thank God, he got shipped out himself, and I grabbed the chance to put in for amphibious training. So here I am, the brand-new skipper of an old barge of an LST. Of course, it's a lot of responsibility, but I love having my own ship and being my own boss."

He was filled with the vernacular that I associated with the early part of the war, enthusiasm at the idea of command, ostentatious disgust with shore duty and the widespread, fallacious assumption that we were all lucky to be "in it." I had no such feelings. I simply envied, without rancor, the men who were comfortably situated at home.

"You're really a big shot now, Victor," I said encouragingly. "I've never had a command. It would probably scare the pants off me."

"Of course, an LST is nothing like a destroyer," he said quickly, trying, in all seriousness, to save my feelings. "I'm under no illusions about that. But then you always *were* ahead of me, Teddy. I can remember how I felt when you made that touchdown against Pulver!"

As I feared, this was only the first item in a Pandora's box of reminiscence. I felt uncomfortable as he talked on with such easy, even eager fluency about our school days. It seemed vaguely indecent to pose such highly particularized chatter against the wide indifference of the Pacific. I had not been happy at Chelton myself, not because, like Victor, I had been hazed and unpopular, for I had always been big and able to take care of myself, but because I had felt inarticulate in the rush of school competition and homesick for my family's farm in Vermont. Perhaps I was maturer than my contemporaries and unable to care as strongly as they cared; perhaps I was simply slow. At any rate I had grown up and left it behind me.

"But you did well enough at school, Victor," I said, with some impatience. "You were an editor of the Lit, weren't you? And a magna?"

"But you can't imagine how hard those things came, Ted," he insisted. "*All* those things. Playing football. Writing leaders for the paper. Making friends." He shook his head sadly.

"Then why did you bother?"

"Because Chelton *makes* you!" he exclaimed, as though it was all very obvious and I was being very stupid. "Every boy at Chelton has to learn to be a *man*." His tone had risen as he spoke, and then he smiled, suddenly and sheepishly. "*I* had to learn, anyway," he continued more calmly. "I had to learn all the things that came so easily to you, Teddy. And I suppose, in my own way, I have learned them. I went to college. I got married. And before the war I had a perfectly respectable job in marine insurance."

He ended on what struck me as an almost defiant note. I thought of the dreary New England school with its Gothic buildings, impersonal and snow-covered, and the endlessly struck note of the future, one's own future, so full of honors and responsibilities, echoing down the long, varnished corridors with all the coathooks and the faded lithographs.

"Then you've done more than I have, Victor," I conceded to him. "I haven't married. And as a matter of fact, I didn't even have a job when I went into the navy."

I noticed the gleam of superiority in his eyes as I said this. But whatever were Victor's satisfactions they did not stay with him. The gleam faded almost immediately.

"Yes, but you don't care, Ted," he said with a little shake of his head, as if coming back to the fact in others that always stumped him. "That's it. If you don't care, you don't have to *do* things." He looked naïvely despondent. "How I envy you that. I've always envied you that."

"Well, you don't have to envy me my quarters here, anyway," I said, to get him off the subject. "How about putting me up on your LST? Till my can gets in?"

He looked surprised. I am not sure that he was entirely pleased, but he could not very well refuse. When I left the club it had been agreed that I would pick up my gear at the BOQ and that he would send a boat for me later that afternoon.

2

At the little pier by the sea-plane anchorage I found an LCVP, at the appointed time, manned by two sailors wearing dirty dungarees and blue-painted caps, which I identified as Victor's by the number, painted on its side, of its parent LST. I dropped my bag in the bottom of the boat and jumped in after it, and the coxswain, greeting me with a nod, shoved off. We plowed our way through the crowded anchorage, past battleships and cruisers, past naval auxiliaries and transports, through endless rows of liberty ships and tankers, but it was forty minutes before we came in sight of the LST's, looking like long fat sea cows, riding placidly and securely at anchor near a small coral island with three palm trees. They were old ships, without the heavier armament of those more recently constructed; their sides were scarred and rusted, and their afterdecks, covered with miscellaneous canvas rigging, gave the effect of tenement porches. They had the comfortable and assured air of veteran fighters; they seemed to say, with a truculent but self-confident air: Okay. So we look like hell. But wait till you've been in this God-forsaken theater as long as we have. Then you can talk. If you're still alive, brother.

When we came alongside Victor's ship, which was the most battered of the group, I climbed up the shaking chain ladder and found him at the gangway to greet me. I saluted him smartly, in recognition of our new relationship, and we shook hands. He was obviously nervous, for he turned away from me almost immediately and leaned over the rail to shout instructions to the boat crew. An officer who introduced himself to me as the Exec, a short, dark man with expressionless eyes and a polite, deliberate way of speaking, showed me into officers' country and to the empty four-bunk cabin that was to be mine during my stay on board. I told him that I was an old friend of Victor's, but he seemed uncommunicative.

Victor came in after a few minutes and took me for a complete tour of the ship from bow to stern, starting at the bow doors and walking aft through the huge empty tank deck to the crew's quarters, then down to the engine rooms, and finally, when my hands were black from gripping ladder rungs, back to the main deck and the wheelhouse and then up to the bridge. His ship was no better or worse than other LST's; it was not very clean, and discipline was obviously lax, particularly to the eyes of a destroyer man like myself, but one felt that it could do what was expected of it. Victor was almost childishly enthusiastic about the ship; he had been through the terrible moments of first taking command and was now in the fine flush of an early confidence.

"I've got a lot to learn, Ted," he told me earnestly. "Nobody knows that better than I do. But the point is I've been in the navy long enough to know what *not* to do. Oh, Ted, if you knew the resolutions I'd taken!"

We were standing on the bridge, leaning on the rail and looking down over the wide deck where the gunners' mates, in leisurely fashion, were cleaning the twenty-millimeters.

"How's your Exec?" I asked.

"Devett? He's okay." His face clouded momentarily. "You've talked to him?"

"I have."

"Did you like him?"

I realized now that I hadn't.

"No," I answered. "He seems like a surly bastard." The navy taught one quick judgments, usually inaccurate.

"He means well," Victor said apologetically. "He's terribly efficient. Only he seems to have a chip on his shoulder about me. He's been Exec, you see, for two years."

"Why wasn't *he* made skipper?"

"That's just it. He didn't want it. Though he was perfectly qualified."

I sniffed.

"One of those," I retorted. "Can't be happy unless he's got a skipper to bitch about. God! There are so many of them."

"But he's a good man, Ted," Victor protested. "Really.

Naturally he gets impatient with me, because he knows so much more than I do. It must be hard to be under a neophyte when you've been practically running a ship for two years."

"Not when you've turned down a chance to be your own boss," I pointed out. "He deserves anything he gets. And he's damned lucky to get you. I'll bet you try to make friends with him the way you used to at school with all the guys who picked on you."

He winced.

"I try not to lose my temper, anyway," he said. "I tell myself every morning that I'm going to be patient with everybody. Even with Devett. Or rather especially with Devett. The other officers are fine. Very young and friendly."

I looked at him and shrugged my shoulders.

"It might work," I said. "Personally, I'd eat his ass out a couple of times. Just for nothing. Then he'd learn to be grateful when you're nice to him."

A bell tinkled from the wardroom; it was time to eat.

3

I noticed during the next couple of days that Victor and the other officers were more congenial when Devett was not around. The Exec was not popular, nor was he held in any particular awe, for authority on small ships is centered in the commanding officer, but he had the constantly felt personality of the sharply sensitive, and his sarcasm, unending and disagreeable, made the others unwilling to bandy words with him unless they were in the mood for a row. He assailed Victor all the time with quiet, acid questions, beginning: "Am I to understand, Captain, that it is to be your policy to — ?" Victor however, took it well, too well. He always gave Devett his reasons and tried to convince him. The other officers appreciated this, but to Devett it was merely a betrayal of weakness. I pointed this out to Victor, but he declined to discuss it.

"I can only do it my way, Ted," he said patiently. "I care more about making a go of this than anything I've ever done in my life. Let me be."

He was certainly not a bad skipper. He was very conscientious and was constantly touring the ship, though with what in mind it was not always clear. The ship had recently returned from an invasion, just before Victor had taken command, and there was very little activity aboard. It was one of those long, sluggish, inert, post-combat periods that could be such a relief for the first few days. Victor was making every effort to send the crew ashore on beer parties but he never went himself. We spent the evenings playing backgammon together. He seemed to have got over some of his embarrassment at having me aboard.

The part that he was playing, as I gradually made it out, was that of the commanding officer who, though aloof and superlatively able, although essentially a lonely creature from the very intensity of his vision and the lofty reaches of his imagination, was still willing, even eager, to respond to the overtures of friendship from his junior officers and to encourage and assist them in every way. I could see by the way he smiled in the wardroom and the way he listened to anecdotes that I knew must have bored him, how consciously he was trying to model himself on the idea of the leader who could lean, with a condescension that was only charming, on the surrounding Horatios — if there were any. Yet even when I recognized this, seeing Victor as I did with the clarity that comes with long separation, I could not quite laugh at him, for Victor had a certain charm, and there was a pathos in the very braveness of his effort — and, after all, it *was* an effort, however fatuous, to do the right thing by people to whom he owed a responsibility — that made the ensuing debacle even more terrible to me than it would in any event have been.

We were having lunch in the wardroom the fourth day after my arrival, when a messenger came in from the gangway with a dispatch slip on which the signalman of the watch had scrawled a blinker message. I saw Victor pucker his brow as he read it and handed it to Devett. Devett glanced at it.

"We're going alongside the APA 680 to get your water, Ellerson," he said to the Chief Engineer.

"At last. What time?"

"Fourteen hundred."

"Isn't that typical!" Victor exclaimed suddenly. "They *never* give us warning! And I've already told the liberty party to be ready at thirteen-thirty. Do you have to have that water today, Mr. Ellerson?"

The young engineer looked at him in surprise.

"Captain, you know how low we are."

"The liberty party can still go, Captain," Devett pointed out. "You won't need them to move the ship. We'll be back at anchor before it's time to pick them up."

Victor was silent for a moment. Then he nodded.

"Make all preparations to get under way, Mr. Devett," he said sharply. "Liberty party report to the gangway at thirteen hundred. Special sea detail at thirteen-fifteen."

He got up suddenly and left the wardroom. It was obvious that he was upset, but the others continued their meal unnoticing, and I said nothing.

The rasping sound of somebody blowing into the public address system, to see if it had been properly tuned up, carried through officers' country.

"Hear this," came a loud screechy voice. There was a pause while the instrument was tuned down. "Hear this," came the voice again, very Southern and barely audible. "All departments, make preparations for getting under way."

As I went out of the wardroom to the gangway to smoke a cigarette by the rail I heard the clanging of the annunciator test. The liberty party was beginning to foregather by the ladder. Looking out over the anchorage I noticed that it was blowing up a bit. Victor came out and stood beside me.

"Wouldn't you know it?" he said irritably. "We lie around doing nothing for two weeks while the sea is like glass. But the moment it gets choppy we have to get under way! Typical!"

This struck me as rather unreasonable.

"You don't call this choppy, do you?" I asked "It's easy to see that your sea duty has all been out here. Where are we going?"

He pointed to an APA anchored half a mile off our port bow. I borrowed his binoculars and studied her for a moment.

"Nothing to it," I said, handing back the binoculars. "We'll be back by four. How about our going to the Officers' Club?"

He looked at me oddly.

"How can I think about that *now?*" he demanded.

I felt rebuffed and surprised, but when he had gone inside this gave way to a feeling of uneasiness. Again the annunciators jangled, and the sound made me jump. I went in through Victor's office to his cabin without knocking and found him sitting on his bunk with his head in his hands. He looked up suddenly when he heard me.

"Vic, what's on your mind?" I asked. "Are you worried about moving the ship? Let Devett do it."

He sniffed.

"Wouldn't he just love that."

"What's there to it?" I asked. "Why does it matter who does it?"

He looked away and shook his head.

"There isn't really anything to it," he said.

"Haven't you handled the ship before?"

"Oh, yes. Not much, but enough. I can do it." He smiled at me reassuringly. "It's just that I always get this way before I do it. And when I sleep I dream about collisions."

"That means you won't have one."

"Hear this," came the voice, loudly and suddenly, over the public address system. "Station all the special sea detail." Victor got up. "Station all the special sea detail," the voice repeated.

"Can I go up on the bridge with you?" I asked. "Do you mind?"

He smiled again and put his hand on my shoulder.

"Oh, I do and I don't, Teddy," he said. "Come on up. It's a funny world, isn't it? Here you and I are alone, except we're dressed in these silly uniforms. It's like Chelton all over again. I thought Chelton was unreal when we were there, like the war and all this, but it's real to me now. Seeing you again makes me feel that. The past *is* real."

"I don't believe in the past," I said firmly. "Or in the future. But if it's going to make you feel as if you were back at Chelton to have me on the bridge, I'll stay here."

He shrugged his shoulders. A messenger appeared in the doorway of the cabin.

"Mr. Devett wants to know if you're coming up, Captain."

"Tell him, yes."

I went into the wardroom and drank a cup of coffee. It was all very well for me to tell myself that in a big war it was fantastic to worry about an LST moving to take on water in a peaceful anchorage, but the fact remained that I wished it was over. I lit a cigarette and went up to stand in the wheelhouse. I could see by the way the ship was swinging that the anchor was already coming in. In the wheelhouse the Chief Quartermaster was standing at the helm, smoking. A sleepy-looking freckled boy was at the annunciators. Up at the bow I could see a small group of men standing around the anchor capstan. Everything gave back the infinite routine of it.

I heard the whistle as the anchor broke ground, and Victor's voice, high and sharp, came through the voice tube.

"All engines ahead one. Right ten."

The annunciators jangled, and the Chief called back: "All engines answer ahead one, sir. Rudder's right ten, sir."

From far below came the muttered throb of the responding engines and, very slowly, we began to move away from our anchorage. I went out on deck and walked about in front of the wheelhouse where most of the other officers were gathered. The annunciators jangled as we increased speed, and, looking ahead, I saw that we were moving smoothly towards the APA which was flying affirm on her port yardarm. Everything seemed to be going easily, and I went up to the bridge and stood in front of the conning tower, well out of Victor's way.

The wind was increasing, and I could see that the APA was swinging and would, if we continued at our present angle of approach, have her stern to our bow when we were close enough to throw the first line. I heard Mr. Devett, who was also navigator, point this out to Victor.

"Yes, I see," he said, and for a few moments he did nothing. I glanced around swiftly and saw the set expression of his face.

"Left to 232," he said at last.

"I'm afraid that won't be enough, Captain," Mr. Devett warned.

"Left to 220," Victor said. "All ahead two."

The stern of the APA was now almost dead ahead. I could hear the Captain's talker acknowledging the reports of the lookouts on the bow. I held my breath.

The Chief in the wheelhouse was a friendly man and on friendly terms with Victor. I heard his voice, gently warning, over the voice tube.

"Do you think you'll make it this run, Skipper?"

Victor who had been staring fixedly ahead at the rapidly nearing stern seemed suddenly to come to life.

"I guess not," he answered through the voice tube. "We'll try another approach. Left full rudder."

I breathed in relief as I watched the anchorage and the islands slip by the rapidly swinging bow.

"I suggest you try a more perpendicular approach, sir," Mr. Devett said. "And turn sharply to come alongside when you're in close. It's the only way you can do it."

Victor, however, did not seem to agree. We turned around and approached the APA once more, this time at slightly more of an angle, and it looked for a few moments as though we were going to make it, when the anchored ship seemed suddenly to stop swinging, and Victor found himself approaching her bow almost perpendicularly without time to turn. We were nearly on top of her when he started backing his engines, and only one line had gone over to the APA. The LST continued to move stubbornly forward, and in another minute we were straddled awkwardly across the bow of the big gray ship. Her long side was dotted with the watching faces of her crew. I heard a squawking sound from above and, looking up, saw a commander standing on the port wing of her bridge and yelling at us through an electric megaphone.

"Stand off for another approach!"

There is no more electric feeling of proximity than when two ships are unexpectedly too close. There is the particular moment when one is suddenly conscious of the noise of the imprisoned water between them and when the figures at the rail and on the bridge of the other become human beings. They become formidable, critical, at the same time, and when it is a larger ship, and with more rank on board, the swift intrusion upon one's own authority and self-respect is appalling. Victor ordered his engines ahead standard, but he put on too much left rudder, and there was an ugly scraping as the LST's starboard quarter slowly pivoted against the sharp bow of the other ship. I saw our stern rail carried away and noticed the gunners mates rushing to the bashed-in gun tub. On the bridge there was silence except for Victor's impatient:

"All ahead full."

Most of the crew was up on deck now to see what had happened, and some of their humorous cracks floated up to the bridge. "This ought to get us stateside." "The Japs haven't done that much in a year!" They had the detachment that comes with Pacific duty; if the skipper was going to bang up the ship, why that was fine. Damage, if bad enough, might mean San Francisco. Why not? The day of routine had become a holiday.

I heard Devett talking to Victor in a low tone, illustrating with his hands what was probably a new plan of approach. Devett looked very serious and was talking fast. He was not a man, I guessed, who desired his skipper's misfortune to the extent of not assisting him. Victor looked very pale and was nodding his head, but I knew that he was not taking it in. I had a sudden image of Victor at school in a debate, standing at the rostrum, his lips frozen in a smile and no sound emerging from his mouth. For minutes and minutes while I had suffered for him. It was as if the mast of the APA had become the Gothic spire of the school chapel.

Again we turned and made our approach to the APA, this time with the crews of both ships lining the rail to observe the performance. I wanted to go below to the wardroom, but I found myself immured to the spot, sick with apprehension. It was so painful that I made a conscious effort to get outside of myself, to try to view the episode as a spectator, to destroy, if I could, the identification of myself with Victor. For a moment I almost thought it accomplished; I folded my arms and fixed my eye on the nearing stern of the APA and said to myself calmly: There. He's done it again. He won't make it, but as we came closer and closer, as it became agonizingly apparent that he really wasn't going to make it, my equanimity vanished, and I clenched my fists and rose to my tiptoes.

I had to look away as we struck the APA's bow again with

our starboard quarter. I heard the derisive, exclamatory shout of our crew and the squawking of the angry commander through his electric megaphone. I looked aft and saw that almost the whole guard rail of the stern gun tub was gone. I could not look at Victor. I left the bridge and went down to the wheelhouse where the Chief was working hard to keep the ship on a course that Victor had just given. He was shaking his head in disgust.

"Mr. Devett is taking the con, Chief," I heard Victor say through the tube. "Steady as you go."

"Steady as you go, sir."

A moment later Victor brushed by me without a word and went into the charthouse. I followed him and saw him go down the ladder to his cabin. Obviously, he did not want to talk to me. I went sadly back to the bridge and watched Mr. Devett bring the ship alongside the APA with what appeared to be the ease and finesse of a masterly ship handler.

Victor locked himself in his cabin, and I was unable to see him that day or the next. I had received word from the base that my destroyer was in, and it was apparent that I would have to leave without even saying good-bye. The atmosphere in the wardroom was subdued and embarrassed. The officers wanted to have a post-mortem on Victor's ship-handling, but they felt a constraint in my presence.

Mr. Devett came to my cabin to tell me that a boat was waiting to take me to the seaplane area. This, I had to concede, was polite of him. He stood there, smiling perfectly pleasantly at me, just as if nothing at all had happened.

"I suppose you'll never let him forget this one," I said as I closed my bag.

"Who?"

I glanced at him irritably.

"Who are you trying to kid?" I asked. "You'll throw this in Harden's face every time you get a chance."

"What makes you say that?"

"Any dope can see that you hate his guts."

Devett's smile vanished, and his eyes glared at me. They were hard and black.

"I don't hate anybody's guts," he said slowly. "Except maybe the guy in the Pentagon who sends an incompetent son of a bitch to play at being skipper of an LST."

I was sorry that I had gone so far. Certainly nothing that I had said to him was going to do Victor any good.

"Look, Devett," I said, changing my tone. "You seem like an all-right guy. Give him a chance, will you? He'll make out. But it's a new job, and he's nervous and needs an exec whom he can count on. You know what I mean."

Devett looked me straight in the eye.

"Then why don't they send him one?" he demanded.

I closed my lips tightly and picked up my bag.

"Damn you," I said. I went out to the gangway and clambered down the ladder into my LCVP.

4

I did not hear from Victor again, directly or indirectly, until the war ended, a few months later. The jubilation that burst over the Pacific on V-J day was equaled only by the lethargy that immediately followed it. The cardinal social rule at every officers' club was that no topic but the "point system" could be discussed; we counted and recounted our points of service and protested the injustice of the system, and if anyone had the effrontery to throw into the discussion some unrelated topic such as the atom bomb or President Truman, fingers would drum on the table until the subject of discharge had been successfully reinstated. I suffered under what I considered the peculiar injustice of being held as indispensable although I had more than the requisite number of points. I would sit inattentively sipping bourbon while others told me of their misfortunes, and at the first opportunity I would introduce my own tale of woe. Like everyone else I had cut my work to the minimum. On the whole none of us were too unhappy. We knew that we would get out eventually.

One day in Guam, two months after the surrender, I went according to habit to the Officers' Club at four o'clock, when it opened. I was looking around for a group when my eye fell on Sam McDowell, a cheerful young ensign whom I remembered as the communicator on Victor's ship. He was sitting on a bench with another ensign whom I did not recognize, and I waved to him. He waved back, and I went over and sat down. It turned out that he was very low on points indeed and had been transferred from Victor's LST to Guam to await further transfer to a ship in Japan. I condoled with him over this and then told him about the unreasonable attitude of my own commanding officer. After these preliminaries I permitted myself to ask about Victor. He seemed surprised that I hadn't heard. Victor, it appeared, had been transferred to Pearl Harbor just before V-J day.

"Is Devett skipper now?" I asked.

"No. He was transferred at the same time. We got a complete new deal."

I finished the paper cup filled with bourbon and Coca-Cola and reached for one of the extras that I had placed in the middle of the table.

"Did Victor ask to be transferred?" I asked.

McDowell shrugged his shoulders.

"I imagine so," he said. "You were on board the time he tried to bring her alongside the APA in Ulithi, weren't you? Well, you remember what happened. We never saw him after that. He stayed in his cabin and let that bastard, Devett, run the ship."

I stared.

"I suppose he came out for meals?"

"Sometimes. But more often he had them alone in his cabin. He sort of abdicated."

I closed my eyes for a second and thought of our graduation and of Victor, in white flannels and a red blazer, under the cherry trees at Chelton. So bright and so hopeful, after the first of his many hurdles.

"Did he drink?" I asked.

"I suppose so. But not so as you noticed it much. The thing is, you didn't notice *him* much. He just wasn't around."

It was still too much for me.

"What do you suppose he did all day in his cabin?"

"Can't imagine," McDowell said, reaching for another drink. "Moped, I guess. I was sorry to see it happen. He hadn't been a bad guy at all before that. But then he got moody, and when he did come to the wardroom, he didn't speak to anybody. He got sloppy. Didn't shave and that sort of thing."

This, with Victor, went a long way towards indicating complete collapse.

"I suppose Devett enjoyed it all."

The ensign shook his head.

"That was funny. He didn't seem to. We all thought he would, but once the skipper had really gone to pieces, he wouldn't hear a word against him."

Well, it was strange. Perhaps Devett, for all his faults, was not a man to go on with the fight when he had won. He may have sensed that the last bucket had been drawn from the well of poor Victor's nervous energy. Or perhaps more simply he felt that the symbolic position of the commanding officer had to be kept up. I didn't know. I didn't want to think, either, of the effect that my visit might have had on Victor. I went to the bar and bought McDowell another drink and then wandered through the crowded tables until I had found a new group to whom I could tell the sad story of my "indispensable" classification.

FINISH, GOOD LADY

Finish, Good Lady; The bright day is done,
And we are for the dark.
—A<small>NTONY AND</small> C<small>LEOPATRA</small>

FINISH, GOOD LADY

"Oh, I know all about you, Miss Delaney," Mrs. Codman declared in her high voice. "You were with old Mrs. Lord. And before that with my cousin, Angeline Trevor. You taught school once at Miss Higby's. And you even once wrote a book. On the girlhood of Queen Victoria. You see, I have my dossier." She shook a little memorandum pad in a tortoise-shell case.

I confess that I was surprised and flattered. The mention of my poor forgotten little book had the effect of completely unsettling me. If you were an old maid who had to touch up her hair to look young enough to qualify as an old lady's paid companion and if you had traveled by bus all the way from New York to Anchor Harbor, Maine, on the strength of a telegram from an utter stranger, you would know how gratifying such things could be.

"Fancy your knowing all that!" I exclaimed.

"Well, you see I don't like to get just *anyone* for Mama," she said quickly. "It's shocking to me how my friends and contemporaries neglect their parents. They seem to think, don't they, that if the poor old things have a drive in the park in the morning and a nap in the afternoon, they should be satisfied? But I am not like that. I *live* for my mother, Miss Delaney."

I watched her carefully as she told me this. She was a tall, bony, handsome woman with a very powdered face and long brown hair drawn straight back over her head and exploding, at the back of her neck, in a huge cluster of tiny curls. I knew that she must be fifty-five, but she did not look it, any more than she looked any age. Her eyes moved back and forth without settling on me, and her hands, long and white like her face, fluttered vaguely at her sides. She seemed, with the exoticism of her Chinese robe and the elaborate affectation of her smile, to be trying to conceal her bigness and her strength. Yet her sentiments were commendable. There was no doubt of that.

"One should certainly look after one's parents," I said approvingly. "Too many people, as you say, forget."

"Well, if we're agreed on that, Miss Delaney," she answered me brightly, "I think we must really be agreed on everything."

When I left the vast living room, so desperately eighteenth century, crowded with porcelain figures of ladies curtseying and little gilt chairs, I went out on the terrace that overlooked the pine trees and the sparkling Maine ocean to breathe in the golden air. I was not at all sure that Mrs.

Codman and I would be agreed on everything, and my prosaic nature was already troubled by the sense of unreality with which the air was so charged, but beggars, after all, are in no position to be choosers. I *had* the job, and it was for the job that I had come.

I had been engaged for the rest of the season as a companion to Mrs. Lorne, Mrs. Codman's octogenarian mother. The great house of stone and shingle belonged, it appeared, to the old lady, and she and her daughter spent the summers of their common widowhood in it together, waited on by twelve maids in an atmosphere of stately and unrelieved femininity. The only representative of a third generation was Mrs. Codman's married daughter, Nora Jones, a taciturn, diffident young woman who lived with her three small children in what had once been a gardener's cottage near the big house. Mrs. Codman never seemed to take any particular interest in Nora; her preoccupation was entirely with Mrs. Lorne whom she looked after with an assiduousness that considerably lessened my own duties.

She took me out on the porch, on the morning after my arrival, to present me to her mother. Mrs. Lorne was sitting in a wicker chair, her shoulders hunched together, her head lowered and her gnarled, jeweled hands clasping a walking stick that was resting against her knees. Her face was long, oval and rather grim; her cheeks and eyelids drooped in a semblance of repose. She made me think of an old lizard basking in the sun; only the frivolity of the red and yellow flowers on her hat, so absurdly out of key with the rest of the picture, gave any evidence of her inner sense of union with Anchor Harbor.

"Mama, dearest, this is Miss Delaney," Mrs. Codman began loudly, leaning down and putting an arm around her mother's shoulders. "You remember that I told you about Miss Delaney, don't you? She's come to read to you and be *such* a friend."

Mrs. Lorne gave me a brief, inhospitable look.

"I hope she's better than that Slater woman, anyway," she said with the irresponsible rudeness that I had come to know so well in the old. "She was always reading me things I didn't want to hear. And mumbling, too. Do you remember how she mumbled, Alix? Like an old frog."

Mrs. Codman smiled her mannered smile and put her head affectionately close to her mother's.

"Oh, Miss Delaney won't mumble, darling," she assured her. "She's a literary lady. She's even published a book. A whole book."

The old lady grunted.

"As long as she doesn't read it to me," she retorted.

"Oh, she won't," her daughter again assured her. "Now we'll just see. Right away. Miss Delaney, would you mind reading Mama a column from the Anchor Bulletin? I have it here. Suppose you read us the social column? That would be so nice." And she handed the paper to me, folded open at the article in question. I put on my pince-nez, cleared my throat and started off in a rather nervous voice:

"The younger fry were all agog last night at the soup and salmon supper that Archie Kriendl gave on board his new motor launch, 'Peg-o'-my-heart' — "

I read on down the column, giving as cheerful an emphasis as I could to each note of its sterile gaiety. I assumed, of course, that it was only a test piece that had been chosen at random from the paper. I was surprised, therefore, to find, each time I looked up at them, that Mrs. Lorne and her daughter were following the reading with a scrupulous attention. As I continued on down through the seemingly endless list of dinners and cocktail parties that went to make up a single day of Anchor Harbor's gay round, I had an odd feeling that the old lady was coming to life. She nodded or shook her head; she murmured indistinguishable little side remarks, throaty with approval, and once or twice she even laughed aloud with a cackling enthusiasm. When I came, with some embarrassment, to a reference to herself as the "grand old lady" of the peninsula, she nodded vigorously several times and cried:

"How very sweet!"

"That *was* dear of them," Mrs. Codman agreed. "And, Miss Delaney reads quite charmingly, don't you think?"

"Oh, quite. Yes, quite."

"I think that will do for now, don't you, Mama?"

"I do, my dear."

I handed back the newspaper to Mrs. Codman and went once more to the terrace to see if the ocean was still there.

2

So, at any rate, my duties began. The days were routine and monotonous, but one in my work has to be prepared for that. Every morning after breakfast I went upstairs to Mrs. Lorne's sitting room to read her the morning gossip column. When I had finished this I read any other social columns in any other newspapers or magazines that might have arrived. On Sundays I had to read her the "cottage directory" of the summer colony, which appeared once a week, revised to embrace new arrivals and departures. It took nearly an hour to read through it, but Mrs. Lorne could not bear to have a line skipped and sometimes wanted whole sections read to her over and over again. At noon we went to the swimming club where Mrs. Lorne sat at an umbrella table on the lawn by the pool and drank a cocktail, while her daughter roved in quest of people to bring over to speak to her. After lunch she rested before her drive with Mrs. Codman along the ocean road. On these drives I always occupied the folding seat and spoke only when Mrs. Codman, whose manners, though artificial, were very good, asked me a question. In the evening the old lady and her daughter either went out for dinner or entertained at home, while I had my supper in quiet upstairs in my room.

I had hoped, at first, despite the difference in our ages, to establish a friendship with Nora Jones, Mrs. Codman's daughter, who did not seem to share her mother's or grandmother's tastes. She gave me, however, little enough encouragement. Physically Nora resembled her grandmother; she was a tall, thin, rather charmless creature, with bobbed hair and hostile eyes that peered over the portcullis of her embattled personality, ready to pour hot pitch on the first intruder. She spent most of her time looking after her children and rarely went out at night even when I volunteered to act as a sitter. She seemed, indeed, to scorn those who dined out.

"Everything in Anchor Harbor is a prelude to the evening, she explained to me once. "Life begins at eight. Your job is to be a sort of masseuse to Granny so she'll be able to sit up at the dinner table and talk right, talk left."

"Wouldn't Mrs. Lorne be happier," I remonstrated, "if she spent some of her evenings quietly at home?"

Nora gave a little snort.

"Do you want to kill her?" she demanded.

It was extraordinary to me that a lady as old and as outwardly grim as Mrs. Lorne could take such an intense interest in the social life of the community. I had imagined that a face so wrinkled and austere must be the sign of thoughts grave and philosophic, yet her mind, far from turning to the gates of a heaven so imminently to be opened, seemed to dwell exclusively on the doors of her neighbors that opened nightly at eight. She had, of course, always, during a long life, dined and been dined, and it was possible that what may have been an occupation incidental to larger things had become, in her later years, an end in itself, a sort of pattern in the continuance of which she found a refuge from senility. Or it may have been senility itself. I could not tell. But what was totally inexplicable to me was Mrs. Codman's seemingly passionate desire to satisfy, at every turn, her mother's peculiar tastes. Every night the two of them, one in black velvet with a pearl choker, and the younger in billowing taffeta and gauze veils, got into the old black town car that was drawn up under the stone port cochère and sped off to their evening meal. When they stayed at home it was only to repay their obligations, and I used to watch from my window as the dark limousines rolled down the driveway to discharge their elderly cargo. The front hall on these occasions, filled with canes and wheel chairs, reminded me of the vestibule of the cathedral at Lourdes, which I had seen when traveling with Mrs. Trevor. Indeed, it was a curious world.

I felt this particularly one morning at the club when I was sitting, as usual, with Mrs. Lorne under an umbrella table as she sipped her noon Martini. This was always a difficult time. The old lady regarded it as a social hour, a receiving time, but, unfortunately, many people who were perfectly willing to dine at her house, where the food and wine were good and the company, from their point of view, congenial, eschewed her table at the club where pleasanter groups were to be found on almost any part of the broad lawn by the pool. Conversation with the old lady was, after all, a fairly heavy procedure, and even the kindest could only regard it as a duty. Mrs. Lorne, of course, was quite unaware of this, and every time a waiter came by she would turn her head and grin up at him thinking him a new caller. I would try to distract her attention with little anecdotes of my trip around the world with old Mrs. Trevor to which she never listened, while Mrs. Codman stalked amid the umbrella tables, gently swinging her parasol, her lips frozen in a wide smile, searching for recruits to bring over "for a word with Mama." On the morning I have mentioned, Mrs. Codman must have been unable to find a single recruit, for she had come back to the table alone and had sat down between me and her mother and was leaning forward, her elbows on the table, making conversation as smoothly and deliberately as if she had been acting as hostess at one of her larger and more difficult dinners. The "social hour," apparently, was sacred, even with just the family present, and I could not help a certain grudging admiration for so granite a will power. Nora was sitting on the grass by our table watching her children as they splashed in the shallow end of the pool. She looked very bored.

"Children!" she would shout from time to time. "Not any further now! It's too deep there!"

Mrs. Lorne and Mrs. Codman were discussing a camp further inland that they were thinking of buying to get away, from time to time, from the gaiety of the summer colony. The old lady seemed particularly enthusiastic.

"There'll be one big cabin," she was saying excitedly, "and a lot of little ones. I think there'll even be one for Miss Delaney, won't there, Alix?"

"Of course, there will, Mama, dear. We couldn't go without Miss Delaney."

"And we'll be able to give picnics," Mrs. Lorne continued. "And have a canoe full of men with fiddles!"

"It'll be such a wonderful place for Mama to rest," Mrs. Codman said, looking at me with her same smile and her wide inscrutable eyes, as if it were to be taken for granted that I, too, cared.

Nora turned unexpectedly from her children.

"And when the life in the woods gets too hectic," she said sharply, "I suppose there'll be camps beyond the camps? Why not? It's a way of spending money, isn't it?"

Mrs. Codman looked calmly back at her daughter without answering. There was just the slightest lift of her eyebrows to indicate that she was in any way ruffled. Then she spied a possible candidate for the table, an old gentleman in tight, yellowing flannels who was hurrying across the flagstones, his eyes carefully averted from our group, and she was up and over the grass in pursuit.

"Spending money?" the old lady exclaimed. "Who's talking about spending money?" She sounded agitated. "It's my money, isn't it? I can afford it, can't I?"

Nora was again watching her children in the pool.

"You're the judge, Gran," she said quietly. "If you *are* the judge."

Mrs. Lorne looked down at her granddaughter vindictively.

"If you wish to talk with me, Nora, I think you might have the ordinary politeness to get off the grass and sit at the table," she snapped. "Your generation is turning into a bunch of nursemaids. And bad nursemaids, too," she added spitefully.

I was shocked at such petulance, even in a woman of her years. I turned to poor Nora, to reassure her with a wink or a smile of sympathy, only to be surprised in turn at the expression on her face. She was staring at the old lady with eyes that fairly glittered.

"If I'm turning into a nurse, Gran," she said in a clear, ominous tone, "perhaps you can tell me whose fault it is?"

"You have a husband, haven't you?" Mrs. Lorne demanded fretfully. "Can't he support you? Has he failed?"

Nora's lips moved into the semblance of a smile.

"Yes," she said coolly. "He's failed. Does that satisfy you, Gran?" There was a sudden tenseness in her tone. "Am I sufficiently humbled now? Am I enough of a beggar for you?"

Mrs. Lorne did not answer. She reached for her half-empty glass, but her hand trembled so that she upset it, and its contents spilled over the table and onto her dress. In the midst of the confusion Mrs. Codman reappeared. Without a word she dropped to her knees on the grass and started to dab at her mother's dress with her handkerchief.

"She wants me to die, that daughter of yours, Alix," Mrs. Lorne babbled in her high, querulous voice. "She wants to cut me up into little pieces and feed me to those ravenous brats of hers!"

"There, there, dear," Mrs. Codman murmured soothingly; "she's simply young and selfish. We're going home now. Come, Mama." She helped the old lady up. As they were going off, however, she turned to Nora and hissed at her in a fierce voice too low for the old lady to catch: "I can't leave

Mama alone for a second, but this happens. Will you *never* give up?"

I stared after them in amazement. I do not suppose that I had ever witnessed a scene so peculiarly distressing to my own ordered sense of how things should be. I turned doubtfully back to Nora.

"You mustn't mind what the old lady says," I said soothingly. "She doesn't mean a word of it. She loves you in her heart, Mrs. Jones," I continued. "She often talks to me about you."

Nora placed her calm, suspicious eyes upon me and smiled.

"Oh, Miss Delaney," she reproved me. "Your immortal soul!"

3

I thought about this scene a good deal during the next few days. It had a lingering effect in my mind that seemed too strong even for its ugliness. It was not so much, I decided, the lack of feeling between Nora and her grandmother that disturbed me. I had lived long enough with the old to accept as a regrettable but obvious fact that their descendants, particularly those of a more remote degree, often regarded their continued existence with an impatience concealed only by caution. What bothered me, therefore, much more, was Mrs. Codman's unhesitating adoption of her mother's point of view as opposed to her daughter's. Nora might not have been an ingratiating young woman, but there was a certain integrity in her plainness of manner and speech that appealed to me. In an atmosphere of abounding luxury she appeared to have no part. She dressed simply and acted, as her grandmother had so harshly put it, like a nursemaid. All during the long sermon in the little church on the following Sunday, as I sat behind the old lady and Mrs. Codman, I reflected on the latter's preoccupation with the older generation. Was it good? Or hopelessly bad? Was it natural? Or was it so abnormal as to be responsible for all of the strange atmosphere in Mrs. Lorne's house; was it like King Lear's abdication, as I used to teach the girls at Miss Higby's, an act that outraged nature and produced the inevitable tragedy of the play? It seemed significant that the minister had taken for his text that morning the fifth commandment.

A few nights later, when there was a conference of Episcopal ministers in Anchor Harbor, Mrs. Codman actually found herself in need of an extra woman for one of her dinners, and I was obliged to attend. I sat in silence during the meal while my elderly dinner companions talked to the more engaging ladies on their other sides, and I speculated on the waste, in a single Anchor Harbor summer, that went into this liturgical round of meals. Afterwards I was sitting alone, away from the other ladies, when Nora came and sat by me.

"How are you enjoying yourself, Miss Delaney?" she asked in her faintly sarcastic tone. "Does it grow on you? They tell me it can."

I shook my head firmly, and she smiled.

"I guess you're safe," she said. "For a little while."

I had been bursting to deplore the whole scheme of life. This seemed to be my invitation.

"Will you tell me something, Mrs. Jones?" I asked, somewhat abashed at my own nerve. "Why do you stay here? You can't like it, can you?"

She looked at me with a detached, amused air. I felt that she was sizing me up. Not so much to see if I was worthy of her revelation as to anticipate my reaction to it.

"It's very simple," she said. "I have no money."

I gaped.

"Not any?"

"Not a red cent," she said casually. "Gran's got it all. She's sitting on the pile. Like an old dragon."

"You shouldn't speak so disrespectfully of your grandmother," I reproached her, trying to re-establish some of the thirty-year difference between us. "When she passes on, she'll leave you your proper share of her estate."

For the first time in our acquaintance I heard Nora laugh.

"Fenella, you're priceless!" she exclaimed, using my Christian name with a bold indifference that was doubly impertinent. "I'd like to keep you in a jar."

"What do you mean?" I asked indignantly.

"I'll let you in on a secret," she continued in the same mocking tone. "This turkey that you've been eating. This moderately good champagne that you're drinking. The servants around us. You, yourself, my friend. *That's* my share."

I stared at her.

"You mean," I said, lowering my voice, "that your grandmother is living . . . beyond her means?"

"Beyond her means!" she exclaimed. "Beyond her ends!"

Most of my former employers had believed that it was wicked to spend principal. I suppose I must have unconsciously adopted their attitude.

"But *why?*" I demanded. "Why does she do it?"

"You don't think she knows about it, do you?" she came back at me. "Why, she'd die at the very idea! No, it's my mother. Darling Mummie. She ladles it out for her, right and left. We romp through the remaining securities. It's quite a romp, too, Fenella." She looked about the vast room. "You'll have to concede that."

I shuddered and looked up at Mrs. Codman. She was talking with great animation to the lady on her right; her eyes were moving back and forth and her white, bare shoulders up and down. Mrs. Lorne, at the opposite end of the room, was leaning way forwards toward her neighbor and shaking her old white head. I could hear the uncomprehending cackle of her laugh.

"You mean your mother's spending *all* Mrs. Lorne's money?" I asked incredulously. "But what will she do when it's used up?"

Nora raised her eyebrows.

"What will it matter? She'll have done her duty. She won't, you see, have let Gran down."

"Let her down?"

"It's Mummie's mania," Nora explained, "that people owe that to their parents. She wants Gran to live splendidly. To the end."

I clenched my fists.

"You must go to your grandmother!" I exclaimed. "You must tell her the whole thing!"

Nora smiled.

"You don't see it, Miss Delaney," she said. "You don't see our situation at all. Gran would never believe me." She shrugged her shoulders. "You ought to have seen by now what I count for in this house."

I shifted uncomfortably in my seat under her steady, compelling stare. She surrounded me with doors that seemed to bang in my face. Yet she gave me, at the same time, a feeling that something was expected of me.

"It can't be any fun for you," I said weakly.

"Fun?" Nora frowned. "With children to educate? And all this going on?" She included the dinner party in a quick impatient gesture. "No, Fenella. I can assure you it's not fun."

I clasped my hands together.

"*I'll* speak to her!" I cried.

"To whom?"

"To your mother."

"To Mother!" she exclaimed.

"To Mrs. Lorne then."

She looked at me, I thought, with the same savage, unexpected contempt that she had shown to her grandmother at the pool. It was as if all the contempt that she felt for Anchor Harbor had suddenly been focused on a single person. And that person, for no greater apparent reason than proximity, had to be myself.

"Do you think she'd believe *you?*" she demanded bitterly. "Her companion? A person who's paid to please her? Who even dyes her hair to look young for her?"

Instinctively I clasped my hands to my head.

"It's not dyed!" I cried. Never had I been so humiliated. "It may be touched up a bit, here and there. I admit it. And you shouldn't speak that way to your elders, Nora Jones! You have no business to!"

But Nora only shrugged her shoulders and got up to move away. For a moment I sat there alone, staring in indignation at her stiff back as she crossed the room. Then, quite suddenly, I relaxed. I even managed a little giggle at the audacity of her candor and at myself for thinking that I fooled people with my silly hair. She was so pathetic, this unbending, proud creature, with her neglected children. One had no business to look for sympathy in her tormented soul. One could only try to help. It may have been absurd for a grizzled old companion like myself, hardened by years of intimate association with the senile, to presume to be of assistance to anyone as young and aristocratic as Nora, but who else was there? It seemed a shame for no one to strike a blow, however inadequate, in her defense. Perhaps I was an old fool, a frustrated mother, anything you will, but few indeed were the households where a young matron was willing, at her mother's dinner party, to turn her attention to me, in front of all the more important friends, and call me impudently by my Christian name.

4

As might have been expected, I watched Mrs. Codman and Mrs. Lorne, in the ensuing days, with a more observant eye. I took a housekeeper's note of the daily profusion of flowers in the dark front hall, the shining white-walled tires on the ancient town cars, the ever-twirling sprinklers on the closely cropped lawn that surrounded the house. I saw all and counted all, but what could a creature like myself accomplish? There was no way, directly or indirectly, in which I could limit the flow of the household extravagance. Once I suggested to Mrs. Codman, when she had summoned me to her room to discuss the plan of the day, that her mother was going out too much. She swung around immediately from the big triple mirror on her dressing table.

"The doctors say it keeps her young," she retorted. "They say it's the best thing in the world for her. I suppose you know more than the doctors, Miss Delaney."

"It's no way for a lady her age to be living," I said with a courage that I hadn't known before.

She got up and walked rapidly back and forth, kicking at the skirt of her dressing gown as she turned.

"I have not employed you, my dear Miss Delaney," she said sharply, "for your social advice." Under the powder was the countenance of a little girl, unjustly accused and passionately defensive.

After this altercation I was more than ever in a quandary. I was sure that I had to do with a woman who was, at least temporarily, in a highly neurotic state; it was obvious that normal arguments would carry little weight with her. There seemed to be nothing to do but appeal to the old lady herself, and this seemed a precarious solution. I did not know whether or not she would understand the issues involved or what she would be able to do about them if she did. But then what could I lose? My job. I thought of Nora stalking the streets looking for a job. Of her little son shining shoes. I think I must have become slightly irrational in my preoccupation. And then one day at the swimming club I heard something that steeled me to my desperate alternative. Mrs. Codman told me, under the umbrella table at the "social hour," that she had decided definitely to buy the camp for her mother. A camp in the woods, twenty miles inland, by a lake. Three large cabins. A hundred acres. Nora came upon me later, sitting there alone.

"You look worried, Fenella," she said, with her usual smile. "As if you'd seen a ghost."

"They're actually going to buy that camp!" I cried.

"Of course. Gran wants to be an eagle scout."

"Mrs. Jones! This can't go on!"

"Can't it, Fenella?" She raised her eyebrows. "Can't it really?"

I rebelled at her suavity, at the sunlit air. I gazed up over the umbrella tables and the shingle roof of the clubhouse at the unreal silhouettes of the distant mountains, cut like backdrops in a children's theater against the blue sky. Life, after all, was not like the Shakespeare tragedies that I had taught at Miss Higby's. There *were* things that could be done, and if no one else would do them, well, then, it was up to the companion. The next morning, when I went upstairs for my reading hour with Mrs. Lorne, I did not bring the newspaper. I arrived a few minutes early in the sitting room that connected her bedroom with her daughter's, and the old lady's door was still closed. I stood there for a moment, breathing hard, until I had got up the courage to go to the boule desk with the spindly, curved legs where Mrs. Codman wrote her letters and pull open, one after the other, the little drawers into which I had seen her, during her daily "business" hour, sticking the residue of her scantily examined mail.

My inner predictions, alas, were more than justified. The drawers were stuffed to the very brim with papers that had been carelessly folded or crumpled and jammed in there, obviously over a long period of time. As my nervous fingers poked about, the contents fairly exploded over the monogrammed elegance of the blotter folder into my lap and onto the floor; bills, bills without limit or classification, stuffed away out of sight and out of mind, letters from law firms and telegrams, warning and agitated, from family friends and advisers. It seemed to me, as I glanced rapidly through this angry mass of paper protest, as though all the outraged feelings of the commercial world, whose rules of prudence and economy Mrs. Codman was so grossly violating, had finally erupted from their long confinement to overwhelm us. I may have been tense with excitement, but I was no longer afraid when I heard Mrs. Lorne's door open nor did I move from my position at the desk.

"What are you doing at my daughter's desk?" I heard the old lady ask sharply. "You know you have no business there." I turned around as she came closer and saw the sudden amazement on her features. "Why, you've been messing it up!" She gave an incredulous gasp. "You must have taken leave of your senses!"

I summoned all my courage for the test.

"I know I've done a terrible thing, Mrs. Lorne," I said as calmly as I could; "and I'm quite aware that you will probably wish to discharge me on the spot. But will you please, for your own sake as well as your family's, look at the papers on this desk? I'm not saying anything about what's in them. I'm only asking you to look at them. Before you buy your new camp!"

She leaned on her cane with both hands and looked at me narrowly. Her stupefaction seemed almost to have turned into curiosity.

"Are you implying," she demanded, "that I can't afford it?"

"I'm only implying, Mrs. Lorne," I said, quailing, despite everything, at the sense which she gave me of my own impertinence, "that you should review your situation."

There was a silence. Then she seemed to recover her old imperiousness.

"It seems to me that for a companion, Miss Delaney," she said in a biting tone, "you're singularly nosey."

I nodded dumbly.

"And now," she continued in the same tone, "will you be good enough to leave this room? If you're *quite* through at Mrs. Codman's desk?"

I turned instinctively to repair some of the mess that I had left there.

"No, leave that!" she said sharply.

I turned again to face her; I pulled myself up defiantly for my final exit, but as I did so I realized suddenly what it was I was seeing in her eyes. It was fear; indeed it was panic. I was so taken aback that for a long moment I felt only the full intensity of her concern. Because she *knew*. Of course, she knew! It was as if she were imploring me desperately to deny what I had seen, as if she believed in some odd, senile fashion, that as long as nobody, even her daughter, knew that she knew, it did not have to be true, *but if I* knew, a stranger, a bleak, alien wind through the air of Anchor Harbor, then her blue sky and blue sea would roll up and crumple like the papers on the desk and on the floor. I hovered there, appalled. I was as afraid now as she.

"Get out!" she cried in a sudden fit of temper. "I told you to get out, you meddling fool!"

I heard her voice still after me as I hurried down the corridor to my own room. Inside I fell on my knees by the bed with my head in my hands, too panic-stricken to think. I have no idea how long a time had passed, a half-hour or an hour, when I heard a knock at my door and went to open it. It was Nora with an odd little smile on her face.

"Have you heard about Gran?" she asked. I shook my head quickly. "She's had another of her strokes. She was sitting at Mummie's desk, of all places, and she'd made the most terrible mess of all her papers. I can't imagine why. She can't see enough to read."

I leaned against the door and gave a little groan. Nora was still smiling.

"Didn't I tell you," she said, shaking her head in mock reproach, "that you could do nothing?"

"Oh, Mrs. Jones," I murmured in a sick voice.

"Don't take it to heart, Fenella," she said casually. "The old girl's always having strokes. Maybe one of these days it'll be the real McCoy. While it's still worth while. If you know what I mean."

I stared at her in horror.

"You devil!" I cried.

For the second time that summer I heard Nora laugh.

"My dear Miss Delaney," she protested, "your emotions, I'm afraid, are beyond me. If there's a devil in this house, are you so very sure it's me?"

5

It turned out that Mrs. Lorne's stroke was a bad one indeed, but she lingered in a state of semi-consciousness. There was no further need for my services, and despite Mrs. Codman's kind protests I insisted upon getting out of the way. I left the house and its atmosphere of hush and trained nurses one early morning, without saying good-bye to anyone. I could not, however, return to New York. I took a room in the village and called every morning at the house for news. I never ventured beyond the huge, dark, antlered front hall where Mary, the waitress, gave me the daily bulletin. It was always the same: Mrs. Lorne was still unconscious, and the doctors said the end might come at any time. I do not know how I lived through those days and nights and the seething tumult of my thoughts.

One afternoon when Mary opened the broad white door I saw Mrs. Codman behind her, in the middle of the hall. Before Mary could speak she called to me.

"Oh, it's you, Miss Delaney! Do come in."

I faltered on the doorstep and murmured an inquiry about her mother.

"No, it's all right, come in." And she came over and took me by the arm. "I wanted to talk to you, Miss Delaney. Mama passed on this morning." She led me through the hall and the darkened living room to the den, talking all the while in the same high, seemingly inappropriate tone. "It's all over, you see, at last. She went very quietly at the end, just as we all would have wished. She never recovered consciousness."

We sat down on the sofa, and I fumbled in my old bag for a handkerchief. My head was spinning, and there were tears in my eyes. Mrs. Codman, however, was very calm, very calm and dry-eyed.

"I know how fond Mama was of you," she continued, "and I want to thank you for your helpfulness this summer. You must come one day and select a piece of china for a keepsake."

Unruffled, poised, deliberate, she seemed even further from reality than before.

"I was no help," I said in a shaky voice, rubbing my nose with the handkerchief. "You did everything for your mother, Mrs. Codman. You were a wonderful daughter."

"I?" She shook her head gently. "I wasn't wonderful at all. I loved my mother, Miss Delaney. It's as simple as that." She ran her hands over the folds of her long afternoon dress, smoothing it down on the cushions. "Very few people love their mothers when they're my age, you know. But that, you see, was the love God gave me to feel. And I know now that God has His own wonderful ways of working out His purpose. We had been living, I must confess to you, extravagantly. Very soon I should have had to have told poor Mama. We should have had to have sold things. It would have been quite terrible for her. Now, on the contrary, everything is as it should be. In some ways, Miss Delaney, you might say it was beautiful."

She looked up in surprise as I stifled a sob, and I pressed my handkerchief desperately against my lips. She interpreted this, of course, as the expression of my grief for her mother, as indeed in a way it was, and she leaned over to lay a sympathetic hand upon mine. I could say nothing, and I sat there stupidly while she tried to console me. She might as well, poor woman, have spared her pains, for I knew how little beauty there was to be for me, in the haunted years that gaped ahead, in having been, however briefly, the unwitting agent of *her* God.

THE UNHOLY THREE

As all the heavens were a bell,
And Being but an ear,
And I and silence some strange race,
Wrecked, solitary, here.

—Emily Dickinson

THE UNHOLY THREE

Nellie Hone, her niece could see, was one who had sucked too long and too greedily at the pap of art. Elida knew her William James, and she remembered what he had said about concerts, that a man should do a good deed, like a boy scout, when the music was over, to avoid the "inertly sentimental condition." Certainly, she thought, as she sat behind the tea tray pouring cup after cup for her large and demanding relative, no apartment in New York could have more vividly reflected Mr. James' "condition." Sentimentality was everywhere, in the piles of old theater programs wadded into the shelves on top of the books, in the clutter of bright colors in wide frames along the wall, Bouguereau angels and chess playing cardinals, and most of all in the trinkets that littered the table by Aunt Nellie's chair, trinkets that she was always fingering and holding up to the sunlight, bits of jade and aquamarine, Greek coins, pieces of ribbon, seashells. Elida shuddered. She had no part in it, wanted no part in it, but what did this signify? Trapped, by herself and by others, she could only peer out from behind the thin barrier of her own unnoticed personality.

For she had been summoned from Maine to New York, summoned by Nellie Hone, as superfluous nieces in country vicarages are summoned to London by the rich and titled aunts of Victorian fiction. There had been, it seemed, a heart condition; there had been flutters and murmurs and moments of panic, but even now, when it had largely passed, Elida found herself somehow committed, somehow indispensable, somehow paid to continue her dreary function of dropping pills in water and arranging shawls, of taking telephone messages and of listening, listening interminably, to Aunt Nellie's tales of the days when singers could sing and painters paint. It was perhaps as well that she was one who could face, with a superfluous courage, the idle passage of her life and the uneventfulness of her twenty-nine years. Yet she saw herself facing it; that was the damnable thing. She was not even allowed to be alone in her own auditorium and to weep at the foolishness of what she heard there; she was compelled at the same time to be a critic and to view the play in the light of a coherence that, somehow or other, *she* would have to make of it.

"Elida, I wonder if you'd be a dear and get me just a touch of whiskey? On the rocks?" Caroline Hone, calling at teatime, had paused in the doorway to whisper before joining Mrs. Hone, enthroned in her big chair across the room.

"I've had *such* a day, and tea wouldn't start to do the trick. Besides which I have a bone to pick with your aunt. And that takes something."

Caroline, who was Elida's age, had married Alexander, Aunt Nellie's only son. She was not a lovable person, arrogant and insecure, but she had brought to the Hone family a replenishment of capital which had been badly needed. Her features were sharp and small and far apart, and there was a proud angularity to her chin that, however distinguished, was hardly winning. She disliked her mother-in-law, and her feeling was reciprocated.

"And how are we feeling today, Mrs. Hone?" she asked as she crossed the room to take a chair beside her. "Pretty spiky? Ready for ten operas and eighteen concerts? I've *never* seen you better, I must say."

Her mother-in-law's eyes, round and piercing, snapped at her from behind the pince-nez. Mrs. Hone was an immensely fat woman with a round, intelligent, immobile face. It was the face of a woman of power and intensity, of high blood pressure and temper and possessiveness.

"And wouldn't I give my eye teeth? Gold and all?" she demanded heavily. But sympathy was not to be extracted from Caroline. "If me liver would ever stop from plaguing me," she continued, shifting into brogue. "Oh, me liver! If it wouldn't jump about so!"

Caroline, however, had other things to discuss. She had no time for whimsical accents or bizarre symptoms. Taking the glass that Elida offered her, without acknowledgment, without even glancing at her, she sipped it slowly, her eyes fixed on her mother-in-law.

"Mrs. Hone," she said after a few moments, in the tone of the prepared and fortified. "If your liver is up to it, and

I hope it is, there's a matter of some concern that I'd like to take up with you."

"Bless me! Shall the old be listed to?"

"I should like to know," Caroline continued, in the same clear tone, though now with the smallest tremor in it, "whether you have reason to believe that your son, Alexander, has been finding the company of some other woman more attractive than mine. By some other woman I am not, of course, referring to yourself, whose company, as I well know, he prefers to all others'."

The sarcasm, the very smugness of her voice was witness to her enjoyment of the shock created. She looked from Mrs. Hone to Elida with a bright questioning air; she seemed to be smiling at the wonder of her own frankness. Elida flushed and turned to her aunt. The latter's jaw was thrust forward, and she was glaring at Caroline.

"Must you discuss such things, Caroline," she demanded, "in front of Elida?"

"Oh, Elida." Caroline threw her a brief smile. "Elida knows all our secrets. Don't you, Elida? I'd like to have her opinion too."

Elida got up nervously and walked to the window. Like a servant, she could be allowed to hear. Mrs. Hone turned away from Caroline; she seemed to be lost in contemplating an object on the little table at her side. She picked it up, a piece of ivory, and held it under the lamp.

"It comes from the tusk of a mammoth," she said in a melancholy tone. "Somewhere in the steppes of Russia in the early paleolithic. There's something you don't know about us Hones, Caroline, for all your cleverness. We're paleolithics. That early air was the air that we were meant to breathe."

"I'd hate to have to depend on Alexander's hunting," Caroline retorted.

Her mother-in-law looked at her, almost with pity.

"Alexander and I were never ones to love our fetters," she said heavily. "If he has put aside his slingshot and is visiting the priestess of a neighboring village, is it up to his mother, whose love of freedom he inherits, to castigate him? Alexander will always come back to his cave."

"Well, when he does," Caroline said bleakly, "he'll find that I haven't put aside *my* slingshot. Or my small stone hatchet."

Mrs. Hone looked at her angrily.

"Why do you suspect my boy?" she demanded. "What are your grounds?"

"My grounds," Caroline replied coolly, "are, as you might imagine in such a case, utterly inadequate. Except to me. Knowing my husband." She smiled a trifle sourly. "A very little goes a long way with a man as stuffy as Alexander. For instance, last summer, when I was away at the Cape with the children, I heard that he was seen dining at a night club, in a corner, with a girl who kept turning her face away from the room. And the other day, when I came back from my visit to Washington, I was going through the pockets of a suit of his that I was sending to the tailor's and came upon two ticket stubs. They were for the Lincoln Theater. Which, as you may know, is where *The Ballad Girl* is playing. I asked him that night if he would take me and he said he'd love to. He said he'd been dying to see it."

Elida, standing behind them and squaring the piles of magazines on the table, stared in horror at her cousin-in-law. Was it possible that he had not explained? She closed her eyes and steadied herself against the table. This was madness. Sheer madness. Facts had to be facts. Of course, it had been Alexander who had taken her to *The Ballad Girl,* the only man who would have taken her to anything, her own first cousin, older and married, taking advantage of his wife's absence to be kind to the poor relative who looked after his mother. What could be more natural? And, true, he had taken her out to dinner, twice — she could never forget it — and every evening, when he called on his mother, as he never failed to do, on his way home after work, he and she used to have a little talk, sometimes with a drink, but it was always *about* his mother. After all, she reflected wildly, he could not know how *she* felt. Or could he? She rested her weight on the table with both hands. She was giddy. Why otherwise, in God's name, should he have kept this from Caroline?

Mrs. Hone shrugged her shoulders, as though scorning to weigh the evidence.

"It could be, you know," she said, "that he doesn't find his cave as enticing as it might be. It could be that he's not the only one at fault."

"Oh, yes. Anyone but Alexander!"

"Look into your own heart, Caroline. Search there."

"*My* heart!" Caroline exclaimed. Her indignation finally exploded. "Are you defending him, Mrs. Hone? Of course, if you think keeping some little slut in a snuggery on the West Side, presumably with my money, is paleolithic, I don't suppose there's any point in our discussing it. To me it's disgusting."

Elida turned away from the magazines and the table. She moved over to the bookshelves and rested her palms against the cool, reassuring backs of the encyclopedia. Somehow, she felt desperately, she would have to find a way to face these things. Real things. Not only observed things. But how could she face them on a plane with Caroline, Caroline who had everything and was enjoying even the possibility of Alexander's unfaithfulness? Or Aunt Nellie, who was worse, with her miscellany of trinkets, worshiping beauty at the expense of all discrimination, of moral judgment, playing first with the ivory and then with a buttonhook?

Mrs. Hone only grunted at her daughter-in-law's remark.

"You may think me an immoral old woman, Caroline," she said, "because I don't go around calling everything I see disgusting. There's nothing disgusting under the sky. There's only life. And there's beauty!"

"I take it anyway," Caroline said getting up, "that you do know something about Alexander's wanderings. And if I'm not being importunate, who, may I ask, *is* this girl?"

Mrs. Hone closed her eyes tightly and shook her head several times.

"I see nothing. I hear nothing," she murmured.

"Mrs. Hone, how am I to believe that?"

"I hear nothing. I see nothing," her mother-in-law repeated stubbornly.

"Well, at least we know where we stand," Caroline said sharply, going over to take her leave. "And at least I've found out that there *is* someone. We're dining with you, tonight, I believe?"

Mrs. Hone shrugged her shoulders. Her eyes were still closed.

"And then to the opera," Caroline continued briskly. "What is it to be?"

The old lady's lips barely parted.

"*Tristan.*"

Caroline smiled ironically.

"How appropriate."

Elida, as she always did, followed Caroline out to the lobby.

"I thought your aunt seemed better today," Caroline said as she put her gloves on. She regarded Elida's pale face and long, loose hair with distaste. "I think our fall weather must be doing her good."

Elida nodded politely, timidly.

"We're all going to the opera tonight, I understand," Caroline continued. Elida, after all, could not quite be treated as a paid companion. "Do you like *Tristan?*"

"Oh, I adore *Tristan*," Elida agreed hastily. "Don't you?"

"I can take it or leave it," Caroline said with a shrug of her shoulders. "It's a kind of dope. Perfect for Mrs. Hone. But I pride myself on being a realist. Of the earth, earthy."

Elida gave her a twisted smile.

"I'm sure of that, Caroline," she said.

"Elida!" came her aunt's voice from the living room. "Elida, will you come back here, please?"

The elevator doors opened, and Caroline, with a nod, disappeared. Elida returned to her aunt.

"Yes, Aunt Nellie?"

"Give me a hand, dear. I want to go to my room." With Elida's assistance she struggled to her feet. "Whew!" she panted. "That girl's visits are always bad news, but this one has laid me flat. I'll need more than my usual nap this evening, Elida. You can bring me a nip of Scotch. To warm me blood." She raised a hand suddenly to her brow. "And she's coming for dinner, too! Oh, me trials and tribulations!"

"But it's not true what she said, Aunt Nellie? It couldn't be!"

Mrs. Hone gave her a sidelong look.

"How should I know?" she snapped. "She doesn't know *who*, if that's what you're worried about. She hasn't even a suspicion. Your old aunt was a lady from start to finish. Don't you agree?"

Elida stared.

"Do *you* know, Aunt Nellie?"

"Do *I* know, Aunt Nellie?", Mrs. Hone mimicked her. "What do you suppose, my little innocent? Do you think having eyes, I see not? Of course, I know. I know," she continued emphatically, and again in brogue, while Elida still stared dumbly at her, "that me pride and joy, the only issue, shall we put it, of this old body, has left the straight and narrow at the behest of a certain young lady. And vicee-versee."

Elida looked into the narrow eyes of the huge old woman and felt her heart go cold.

"And who is this certain young lady, Aunt Nellie?"

"Who indeed?" her aunt reiterated, again mimicking her astonishment. "Who, I wonder? Oh, Caroline doesn't know, I grant you. But then she's stupid. She can't see what's under her nose. And I won't tell her, either. Never fear. But *I* know. And you know, too, you foxy creature. Who's the little baggage that's been waiting so shamelessly in the front hall to tempt my virtuous boy when he's calling on his old sick mother? Who's that, I'd like to know?"

Elida's hands flew to her cheeks.

"Aunt Nellie!" she cried. "It's not true!"

"Pish, tush!"

"It's not true," she repeated wildly. "It's not!"

"Neither do I have pain in me joints," Mrs. Hone retorted. "Neither is *Tristan* a beautiful opera."

Elida turned away, speechless, shaking her head violently. Mrs. Hone, watching her, seemed to relent.

"Elida, my child," she said more gently, putting a heavy hand on the girl's shoulder, "you don't think I'm angry with you, do you? Or that I disapprove? You don't think your poor old aunt has gone over to the Philistines after all these years? Oh, Elida!" she protested as her niece only continued to shake her head. "Look at me, my child. Look at your old aunt and tell her all about it."

Elida was shrinking from the unwelcome prospect of these confidences when she heard the doorbell. She knew that it would be Alexander, and she knew her aunt well enough to be sure that she would pick just such a moment for a general clarification. Picturing the horror on his face, she fled out of the room and down the hall to the front door. She threw it open and saw him standing there. With his black derby in one hand and his newspaper folded in the other. He emerged from the subway after a day in the office as neatly pressed and starched as when he went into it. She gazed with a pleasure that was almost painful at the round face over the stiff collar, the thick, brushed hair and the large, timidly sympathetic eyes.

"Your mother's resting," she whispered. "Had you forgotten? You're coming here for dinner. In three quarters of an hour."

"Oh." He glanced in dismay at his gold pocket watch. "I forgot. I'd better hurry home and dress or I'll catch it from Caroline. Tell Mother we may be a bit late."

"Not too late," she warned him. "It's *Tristan*. You know how she is about *Tristan*."

"And how you are about it," he added politely, smiling.

"Oh, me," she said deprecatingly.

"Yes, you," he repeated, nodding. "I know that with you

it's the best or nothing. I don't forget how you were at that musical we went to the other night. You didn't like it."

She gazed at him, her mouth half-open. Did he mean — but no, he couldn't. She took a quick breath and recovered herself.

"No, I loved it," she protested.

He bowed and turned back to the elevator.

"I'll see you at dinner," he said.

That was all, she reflected as she closed the front door after him, but when, for that matter, had there been anything more? He was fond of her, undoubtedly, for Alexander was fond of all his cousins, even the ones from Maine, and he found it enjoyable to chat with her after calling on his mother, preferring, perhaps, her silent admiration to Caroline's caustic tongue. This was little enough, to be sure, but it was all that her imagination had needed for a consolatory, a unilateral romance, something to dream about in the unvarying routine of her days and nights. At least it had been her own and no one else's. And that any part of it should have escaped beyond the thick private walls that she had built so sturdily around it was not merely inconceivable. It was a nightmare. As in a dream she returned to the living room.

"I think I need a nap too, Aunt Nellie," she said. "*Tristan* is such a long opera."

Her aunt grunted.

"Not for those as love it," she retorted. "Not a whit too long."

2

Alexander and Caroline returned to his mother's for a hurried dinner before the early curtain of *Tristan*. They all went straight from the table to the car, and the evening's "ordeal," as Caroline called these family opera parties, was under way. Mrs. Hone's old Packard, "Cousin Tillie," moved through the wet night with a cohesive smoothness and a firm dignity exemplified in its high top, its white-walled tires, and the fat, black-gloved hands of the chauffeur on the thick rim of the driving wheel. They drew up to the curb at exactly the same time as on other nights, and amid a general unraveling of canes and capes, of opera glasses, of librettos and small accessory cushions, Mrs. Hone was assisted to the pavement whence she wended her slow way, supported by her son and daughter-in-law, across the crowded lobby to the ancient ticket collector at the inside door who greeted her as over a sea of new and unwelcome faces. Elida followed in their wake, carrying the inevitable steamer rug required for her aunt's knees, an ancient and heavy piece of material called "Maggie" in line with Mrs. Hone's habit of giving names to familiar, inanimate objects, a kind of animism, designed, no doubt, to keep at bay the hostile spirits of death and vacuity that might otherwise inhabit lifeless things. Elida felt at these times an accessory herself, dragged along, like one of those big, awkward, ridiculous, overdressed French dolls and given, for kindness' sake, a name as appositely inappropriate as Elida. They went up the stairway to the second level and down the corridor to the little plush anteroom of their box where they deposited the paraphernalia of wraps and props. As Alexander pulled aside the red curtain for his mother, Elida could see over the filling house to the great yellow curtain on the stage, but her view was almost immediately blotted out by two old maids in red velvet with small seed pearls, in black pumps and fur neckpieces, who had been sitting in the back of the box and who jumped up now to thank their arriving hostess for sending them tickets and to comment with little screams on some improvement in her appearance, apparent only to them. They were the Misses Harcross; they were "dears"; for six decades they had lurked in the backs of boxes and adored opera. And now as Alexander went through his usual routine of urging them to go into the front row they responded with their usual demurrers: "Oh, no, thank you so much, dear Alexander, but you must sit there with your lovely wife where everyone can see you. My, my, the way you young men have to work downtown, it's a wonder that you ever see your wives at all!" They settled themselves at last in the second row, and Elida could shrink unobtrusively into the desired seclusion of the back corner. Mrs. Hone, however, always arrived early; only a few members of the orchestra were tuning up, and there was time, too much time, for the exchange of programs, the examination of librettos, the testing of opera glasses, for general chatter. Elida felt her nerves grow tense; she twisted her program tighter and tighter and nodded dumbly to the Misses Harcross, longing for the dimming of the lights with a passionate longing. And then, just as she was wondering if she could, after all, bear it any longer or if she would have to flee to the solitude of the ladies' room, came the sudden, blessed relief of the lowering lights and, after a few moments, the harsh, yearning sadness of the opening motif of the Prelude. Her taut muscles could then relax, little by little, and as her eyes closed and she leaned her head against the back of the box she could find the release that she had been gasping for in her tumbled sense of waves breaking along a long coast and of her body, inert on the sand, being rolled and turned and, ever so gradually, drawn out into the liquid nothingness of an infinite sea.

It was not to Elida the music of love, but the music of

longing, longing for escape or submission to the patternless, for death, if you will, or the womb, for peace, for irresponsibility. After a while, when she was again at rest with herself, she could open her eyes and gaze at the others in the box without fear, at Aunt Nellie, moving her big arm up and down to the music, nodding her head, wallowing in it, at Caroline, staring straight ahead, watching, never listening, at Alexander, sitting erect but lost in his own preoccupations. It was only at the opera, he used to say, that he could really think. At such moments she was their equal, even their superior, even Alexander's. She closed her eyes again and hardly reopened them until the sailors were calling their "Heave-Ho!". Brangaene parted the lovers as Mark entered, and the curtain fell. The lights blinded her.

"There's nobody like her," Mrs. Hone was saying, shaking her head. "Not since Ternina."

"Ah, Ternina!" twittered the sisters. "Who was ever like Ternina? These poor young people can't remember those days. But we were Nordica fans, too, weren't we, Nellie?"

"But Ternina! She was all magic."

Alexander promptly left the box for the bar, and Caroline scanned the rows of the orchestra with her opera glasses. Mrs. Hone offered everybody chocolates from one of the packages that Elida had brought. Then the curtain behind them was pulled aside, and Mr. DeLancey, a tall, spare gentleman in his upper thirties, with absurdly narrow wrists and ankles, with long thin hair and an aquiline nose, came in to call on Mrs. Hone. He was her cousin and never failed to do this. He bowed to Elida and to Caroline and just touched Mrs. Hone's hand. He took Alexander's vacated seat and discussed the health of other cousins less ill but also less brave than herself. Then, to Elida's surprise, he turned to her.

"You and I, Miss Rodman," he said with a friendly little smile, "are persons of varied taste in the field of music. Is that not so?"

She stared at him blankly.

"I was referring," he continued with a twinkle, "to my glimpse of you, a fellow Wagnerian, at a musical comedy the other night. Or possibly it was what they now call a 're-view.'" He was addressing himself, not only to Elida, but to Mrs. Hone and had, therefore, he obviously felt, to elucidate any reference to a form of entertainment of which she would probably have never heard. It was only then that Elida saw what was coming and looked down, panic-stricken, at the crushed program in her lap. "I was taken the other night," he continued with the remorselessness of the unknowing, "to a benefit performance of *The Ballad Girl.* It was there, Cousin Nellie, that I recognized your niece. Has she confessed to you that, like me, she has a taste for lighter, gayer music?"

Mrs. Hone did not like to be taken for granted or to have it carelessly assumed by younger relatives that she had no interest in simple pleasures.

"It's very good. I've seen it twice," she lied abruptly.

Everybody murmured politely at this further manifestation of her eclecticism.

"Cousin Nellie, you're wonderful," Mr. DeLancey said promptly. "You don't miss a thing."

And then it came. Caroline's irritable drawl cut across the conversation.

"I wonder if I might ask you, Elida, who took you to this

'review,' " she demanded, turning around in her seat. "Was it by any chance that fellow Wagnerian, my husband?"

Elida made herself look up and face those eyes, those sharp, surprised eyes.

"Why, yes," she almost whispered. "I don't know who else would take me."

She had a sense of the box rocking as Aunt Nellie came to her rescue.

"And why not, Caroline?" she demanded. "Wasn't it a good cousinly act on my boy's part?"

"Certainly." There was an ominous brightness in Caroline's tone. "It's just that I'm envious, that's all. *The Ballad Girl* happens to be something that I particularly wanted to see myself. As I believe I told you this afternoon. In my naïveté."

"But you were away, Caroline," Elida said hurriedly. "I'm sure Alexander would love to go again. It's well worth seeing twice."

Caroline gave her a look that would have put a kitchen-maid in her place.

"Perhaps," she answered coldly. "Except, of course, that I wouldn't dream of asking him. Now."

Elida bowed her head. It was not for her to make suggestions.

"You go to every play in the season, Caroline," Mrs. Hone said roughly. "Poor Elida has no fun at all, cooped up with an old woman like myself. You know what I should like?" She turned to Mr. DeLancey. "I want to include you in this, too, Winthrop," she said. "I'd like to send all of you young people to a night club after the opera. The four of you. I doubt if Elida has ever been to one."

If there were limits to Mr. DeLancey's enthusiasm, there were none to his cousinly co-operation.

"I should be delighted," he said with a bow.

"Aunt Nellie, please . . ." Elida was beginning.

"You'll do as you're told," Mrs. Hone interrupted gruffly.

"Mrs. Hone," Caroline protested, "it doesn't seem to me, from what I've been hearing about musical comedies tonight, that Elida's evenings have been so terribly neglected. Not to the point, certainly, of our all having to stay up late and bore ourselves to death."

There was a pause in which even Caroline seemed to sense that she had gone too far. The corners of Mrs. Hone's lips drooped, and she looked away from her daughter-in-law.

"I'll speak to Alexander," she said in an injured tone. "We'll see if he'll deny his old mother."

The lights again mercifully dimmed, and on the stage in a garden of blue and green, a veiled Isolde chided Brangaene for her fears. It was the scene of night and the loss of awareness, the scene that Elida loved above all, but now there were no Tristans or Isoldes on the stage for her. Between her and the music had come the look of incredulity on Caroline's face, the startled look that had seemed to say: "Not *you*, for God's sake!" Not her. Not Elida Rodman! What earthly fun could it be to be jealous of Elida Rodman?

Yes, she saw it now, put it together. Caroline believed it; that was the incredible thing. And Aunt Nellie believed it. And Alexander? Did he believe it? Did he even know how she felt? Probably, for he would assume, would he not, that anyone in her position of dependence would necessarily fall in love with a man of his class and generosity. And, after all, she reflected bitterly, was he not right? She closed her eyes and clenched her fists and prayed that the awful fear would not be too much for her; she tried desperately to reason with it. If Caroline and Aunt Nellie wanted a woman in Alexander's life to satisfy their craving for drama, was it not true that he, too, wanted a part to play? Why else, in heaven's name, should he have made a mystery of their harmless evenings? She was being called from the wings, that was it; the leading lady was ill, and this was to be her chance. She had learned the lines, God knew, often enough. But why, she broke in almost angrily upon her own rationalization, did they all three look to her so inexorably, why did they, with all that God had showered upon them, have to depend on *her*?

At the end of the second act everybody left the box to stroll except Elida and her aunt. Even the Misses Harcross rose to stretch their legs and went to call on old Mrs. Strickland, a cripple, in a neighboring box. Mrs. Hone remained huddled in her front corner, and it was not until almost the end of the intermission that Elida noticed that her eyes were closed and that she seemed to be breathing with difficulty.

"Aunt Nellie," she asked, going over to her, "are you feeling all right?"

Mrs. Hone looked at her glassily.

"Go with him," she said heavily. "Go off with him."

"Aunt Nellie, what on earth do you mean?"

"You see how she treats us," her aunt continued. "You see what she thinks of us. She hates us. Free him, Elida! Take him away. Don't let her *win*."

Elida felt dizzy, and the heads in the orchestra seemed to come together in a lump and then leap apart. She held her breath for a moment.

"But you forget that he's not mine to go off with, Aunt Nellie," she said in a clearer tone. "He has children. He has responsibilities."

Her aunt only grunted.

"Love," she sneered. "It wasn't that way when I was a girl. My Aunt Augusta gave up everything for Prince Mantowski. It's the world well lost, Elida. Or can't you younger people understand things like that?" She shrugged her shoulders. "And you pretend to like *Tristan*."

"But I haven't had a love potion," Elida reminded her desperately, trying to make light of it. "You will remember that Isolde behaved quite respectably before that."

Mrs. Hone sniffed.

"That's why I'm sending you to a night club."

Elida retired hastily to the back of the box as the others came in and sat perfectly still during the third act of the opera. When it was over and she was assisting her aunt into her velvet coat and when Mr. DeLancey had appeared, opera cape in hand, at the door of the box, Caroline and her mother-in-law faced each other again over the issue of the evening's further entertainment.

"You can have the car to go on to the night club, Caroline," Mrs. Hone said, her face flushed with the effort of getting into her coat. "I can go home in a cab."

Everybody burst into protest.

"It's all right. I'll go with her," Elida said hastily. "I can find a cab."

"You're going to a night club, Elida Rodman," Mrs. Hone said sharply. "And you're going to like it."

"Please, Aunt Nellie."

"Do come with us, Elida," Caroline said unexpectedly. "Don't spoil the party."

Caroline and Alexander had been having a whispered discussion in a corner of the anteroom in which Alexander, curiously enough, seemed to have prevailed. The night club venture had become an accepted fact, and they all appealed to her.

"Don't be a wet blanket, Elida," Alexander said.

"I say, Miss Rodman," Mr. DeLancey murmured.

Elida looked from her aunt to Caroline and from Caroline to Alexander. They were united suddenly in their absurd dependency upon her, and as she sensed it for the first time to the full, sensed it with all its odd responsibilities as well as the peculiar and unfamiliar feeling of superiority that it suddenly gave her, she drew herself up and almost laughed. The moment of silence had become embarrassing. When she turned from them and threw her coat around her shoulders, it was with an air of positive sophistication that she said:

"Well, of course, if you really want me. I couldn't dream of spoiling the party."

It was finally agreed that they would all accompany Mrs. Hone home in "Cousin Tillie," all, that is, except the Misses Harcross for whom Alexander procured a taxi, an old and reliable taxi, of course, from the window of which, as it started off, they continued to pour forth the unquenchable stream of their gratitude, until, out of earshot, they were reduced to the fluttering of hands and handkerchiefs from the back window. Nobody talked in "Cousin Tillie" except Mrs. Hone who told a rather long story about a temperamental Isolde who had thrown her shoe at the conductor, which lasted for several minutes after they had drawn up before her apartment house. When she finally got out it was with many injunctions that they should enjoy themselves and forget about an "old sick woman," and she tucked a ten-dollar bill into Alexander's pocket, insisting that it was to be her party. She was barely inside the building before Caroline took over.

"We'll go to the Ringlade Club," she told the chauffeur. "I want to hear that new French woman," she added to the others. "And, Alexander, I'm delighted your mother slipped you that ten spot. I shall be needing some cigarettes when we get there."

The Ringlade Club was very crowded, and they had to wait in the lobby for twenty minutes before they got a table, despite the fact that Caroline went twice to the headwaiter to explain who she was and who she had been before her marriage. They finally obtained one, in a far corner, and the girls sat on the leather seat along the wall. Mr. DeLancey sat opposite Elida; he unfolded his napkin carefully on his lap, as if he were at a dinner party.

"I'm a great admirer of your aunt's," he began politely. "There's nobody in our generation who has the character and individuality that she has. Oh, I know, of course, what people say nowadays about her contemporaries. That they lived in a narrow world and had no social consciousness. And there is some degree of truth in it." His beaming countenance included Elida in the circular spotlight of their own joint emancipation. "But, say what one will, they looked after their own responsibilities. They had their standards, and they lived up to them."

Elida had heard her mother talk a lot of responsibilities when she was young. She had thought of them as heavy gold objects, triangles and cigar cutters, like those that her late uncle, Mr. Hone, had always worn on his watch chain. Alexander now wore them on his.

"Does having standards," Caroline broke in, "involve rushing through dinner without a cocktail to get to the Metropolitan before the asbestos curtain goes up?"

"Darling," Alexander protested gently, "I distinctly heard Mother ask you if you wanted a cocktail and you said no."

"Well, you know what happens if I say yes," she retorted. "Fume and fuss, fume and fuss, and finally, after an interminable delay, that ancient maid emerges with a silver tray and one very vermouthy Martini. With a cherry in it."

"Darling, that's not fair."

"Oh, who cares?" she said impatiently. "Let's not discuss it, for heaven's sake. Why don't you take Winthrop over to the bar for a moment, and get yourselves a quiet drink while I talk to Elida? We have a little private matter to discuss."

Alexander got up obediently and went off to the bar, followed by the reluctant Mr. DeLancey. Caroline did not look at Elida when they were gone. She stared straight ahead at the dancing couples on the floor, puffing slowly at her cigarette.

"I don't so much mind your borrowing my husband, Elida Rodman," she began in the drawl that she affected when she wished to be unkind. "As long as it's entirely understood between us that I shall be wanting him back."

Elida only looked down into the white emptiness of her plate.

"There are a lot of things that I could say that I won't," Caroline continued. "I think it might be enough if I pointed out that you were employed to be his mother's companion. Not his."

Elida still said nothing.

"Did you hear me?" Caroline said more sharply. "I'm speaking to you, Elida."

She is waiting, Elida thought. Waiting and impatient. Waiting, like Aunt Nellie, and perhaps even like Alexander, for Elida Rodman to play her part. There was something almost pathetic about them, something petulant and childish in the way that they sat so stolidly in the center of the first row and clapped their hands and stamped their feet because of the delay in her appearance.

"Do you deduce all this, Caroline," she said at last, "from the fact that Alexander, who happens to be my first cousin, was kind enough to take me to the theater? Once? While you were out of town?"

"You may have heard of archeologists," Caroline said coolly, "who are able to reconstruct the skeleton of a dinosaur from a single bone of its toe. There you are. Except that my discovery turns out not to be a dinosaur. It's a very small mouse."

The petulance of Elida's audience was turning into something rather ugly.

"A mouse," Caroline repeated harshly. "Don't pretend that you haven't heard me."

Elida gave herself just a moment longer to rehearse her part. Her lips moved as she reviewed her lines. Then she drew a deep breath and turned to Caroline with a courage of which she had never dreamt herself capable.

"All right, Caroline," she said calmly, "I *have* heard you. I was only debating whether or not you were capable of discussing this matter as a civilized woman should. On the whole, I think you are."

Caroline's eyes widened at her boldness.

"Thank you!"

"It so happens," Elida continued, and her heart ceased to pound as she achieved her stride, "that Alexander and I have fallen in love. Very deeply in love, I fear. What will come of it or what we do about it will depend, I must suppose, very largely on how broad an attitude you take."

She watched the shadow of fear follow that of incredulity across Caroline's countenance.

"You must be mad!" she exclaimed. "Alexander may have shown you some attention, I grant. He may even have slept with you, for all I know. The Hones are queer people. But you can't seriously think that a man like my husband would want to go on with this?"

"And why not, Caroline?"

"Why not?" Caroline's eyes bulged. "My dear Elida, you don't think Alexander would leave his wife and children to run off with a country cousin from Maine? If you do, let me tell you that you don't know him."

Elida was feeling some of the intoxication of a first appearance behind the footlights.

"It won't do you any good to be abusive, Caroline," she said, in a lofty tone. "Surely you owe it to yourself to be rational."

"Rational!" Caroline almost screamed. "You have the nerve to say that I should be rational!" She had to interrupt herself, in sheer exasperation, to swallow. The pause, however, seemed to give her time to reflect on her own position. "We'll see who's the most rational," she continued, after a moment, in a more controlled tone. "Let us suppose Alexander were to go off with you. How would you live? You're probably too much in the clouds to face the realities of life. But allow me to elucidate, Miss Rodman. The money we live on is all mine. Every bit of it. Alexander has nothing besides his wretched salary from the bank which would, I presume, be discontinued after his romantic departure from this city with you. I'm not saying that Mrs. Hone doesn't have some mouldy remnant of an old fortune, but I can assure you that she doesn't even attempt to live on her income. The chances are excellent that she'll die broke."

But Elida only smiled.

"That kind of thing, Caroline," she said, "means less than nothing to Alexander and me."

"To you, possibly," Caroline retorted. "You've always been a pauper. But Alexander, I think you'll find, is a horse of a different color."

"Ask him!" Elida exclaimed with a wonderful defiance. "You'll see!"

Caroline's eyes followed hers to where Alexander and Mr. DeLancey were approaching their table across the dance floor.

"Ask him!" Elida repeated.

The men seated themselves at the opposite side of the table, but Caroline simply sat and stared at her husband. Her eyes were wide with an incredulous fear.

"Caroline!" he said. "Is there something wrong? Why do you look at me like that?"

"Elida says you're in love with her," she broke out suddenly in a harsh, rasping tone. "She says you want to leave me and go off with her. Is that true?"

When Elida saw his expression of horrified astonishment she awoke at last to what she was doing. For a moment she quailed; for a second she was almost ready to throw herself upon her knees and beg their forgiveness and retire forever to the desired oblivion of Maine. But at that very moment she was suddenly aware of the drawn face across the table, the unbelieving countenance of the forgotten but nonetheless present Mr. DeLancey, surveying the litter of a whole mantelpiece of lares and penates swept recklessly to the floor, and she was seized with an almost hysterical impulse to laugh.

"Elida!" Alexander exclaimed when he had caught his breath. "Elida, what have you been saying? Have you taken leave of your senses?"

"I've said that we're in love!" she exclaimed defiantly. "Are you ashamed of it? I'm not!"

His eyes bulged.

"Caroline, she must be sick," he said, turning to his wife. "Perhaps she's overstrained. Or tired. You must know there's not a word of truth in what she's told you. She doesn't know what she's saying herself. Caroline, you *must* believe me!"

It was all over, then, in a moment. Elida saw the flood of relief that engulfed Caroline's countenance and knew that her little scene had been played. When Caroline turned and spoke to her husband, her tone was still sharp and cross, but it was now, for the first time, the tone of a woman speaking to a man.

"I should think the poor girl might be overstrained," she retorted, "seeing you every afternoon and having no idea, probably, what your intentions were. I can't blame her for a moment. Living in that extraordinary atmosphere with your mother and hearing all that sentimental drivel that you and she talk about. Paleolithics! Elida, dear," she said turning back to her, "I tell you what we're going to do. We're going to forget all about tonight. We're never going to mention it again. And I'm going to suggest to Mrs. Hone that she give you a vacation and perhaps send you on a trip. With pay."

Caroline's eyes snapped with the excellence of her own

arrangements. Where would they be, after all, these Hones, these fumbling but not unlikable people, these Hones and Rodmans, without her? Alexander sat there in utter docility, grateful for her handling of the situation, dazzled by the revelation of Elida's feelings. It flashed through Elida's mind, even in this moment of crisis, that he ought, good husband though he was, to have given her more than the timid glance of affection that he did. But they were stingy, these Hones. That she surely knew. Well, what did it matter? She had succeeded. They had had their drama, Alexander and Caroline, and they were together again.

"I can see I've ruined the party," she said, reaching quickly for her purse and handkerchief. "You will all understand, I'm sure, if I try to lessen the general embarrassment. By leaving now."

"Elida, we'll take you home," Caroline said, firmly and protectingly. "Won't we, Alexander?"

"Of course, darling."

"That would only make it worse, Caroline," she said hastily. "Mr. DeLancey will be a saint." Her eyes appealed to him. "He will take me home."

Mr. DeLancey, true to his forebears, rose gallantly to his feet. It was not to be expected, after the revelations that he had been forced to hear, that conversation would be lively in the cab. They sat silently in their respective corners, and Elida, stealing a glance at him from time to time, noted that he was staring straight ahead, holding his umbrella upright between his knees. He was keeping himself in readiness, she supposed, to ward off any attack on his virtue that might well be made by the abandoned woman at his side. Yet when the cab had stopped before Mrs. Hone's apartment house and he had got out and was holding the door open for her, his opera hat in hand, he spoke to her with a kindness that she had not anticipated.

"Please let me say one thing, Miss Rodman," he said earnestly, "before you go in. We all have our disappointments. Most of the time we can keep them to ourselves. But not always. Tonight was *your* night. It was a secret that you may rest assured I will always guard."

For the first time that evening Elida felt in danger of breaking down. For all his sarcasm and for all his manner, he at least did not worship the substance under the form. He knew his Hones.

"Oh, Mr. DeLancey," she protested, "you don't understand! Things aren't the way I made them seem tonight at all. I did something very wrong. You see — well — I'm a very complicated person."

"I know, anyway, that you're a very nice one," he said.

She had no wish to embarrass him further by drying her eyes before the doorman. She nodded and hurried into the building. All of the exhaustion of her effort had now descended upon her, and she was hardly able, when she emerged from the elevator, to fit her key in the door. Inside she was hurrying down the passageway to the feverishly anticipated solitude of her own room when she heard her aunt's voice.

"Is that you, Elida?"

"Yes, Aunt Nellie." She stopped and opened the door and gazed in at the huge pile of white on the bed that loomed through the darkness.

"Well?" her aunt demanded. "What happened? You don't think I've been able to sleep a wink, do you?"

Truly, they were inexorable. Elida braced herself for the final effort, the last of her curtain calls.

"What would you have had, Aunt Nellie?" she demanded. "Would you have had him turn his back on his family and his prospects? So that *you* could laugh at Caroline?"

"Listen to the child!" her aunt exclaimed impatiently. "Never mind what *I* wanted. What *happened?*"

"Alexander and Caroline went home," Elida answered calmly. "Together. As they should have done. And as I, too, am going home. As I should do."

There was a pause.

"And who, may I ask, is going to look after *me?*" Aunt Nellie asked peevishly. "Or didn't you young people have time to think of that?"

"Caroline."

"Caroline!" The voice turned to a wail. "You leave me to Caroline! Lay me old bones on the sand for the hyena! This is gratitude, Elida Rodman!"

"Among paleolithics, Aunt Nellie," Elida said, "there *is* no gratitude."

As she closed the door between herself and the blinking mass on the bed, as she at last dropped the big curtain upon her own performance, she felt wrung out and exhausted. Yet there was still a remnant of her earlier exhilaration that had survived the end of the piece, and she wondered, with a strange new bound of her heart, as she walked down the long corridor to her own bedroom, whether it might not take her further than simply to her home in Maine.

THE AMBASSADRESS

> But I —
> I arrange three roses in a Chinese vase:
> A pink one,
> A red one,
> A yellow one.
> I fuss over their arrangement.
> ——Amy Lowell

THE AMBASSADRESS

It was during a very hot August, just a year after the end of the war, while Gwladys Kane and I were enjoying the sun and sand on the Lido, that I received a cable from my sister, Edith, saying that she had decided to come to Paris if she could meet me there. My brother-in-law, George Maclean, the Judge, had been attending a bar association conference in London, and they had three weeks before their sailing date to New York. Diana, George's niece, was with them.

"Why can't they come to Venice?" Gwladys protested. "It's horrid and sticky in Paris now."

We were sitting on the beach, partially covered by an umbrella, for Gwladys was afraid of the sun's effect on her white limbs.

"Edith wouldn't care about that," I said. "Besides, she prefers a place that represents a compromise on both sides."

"A compromise?" Gwladys queried. "You sound as though you and she were going to negotiate a treaty."

"Well, isn't that just what we are going to do?"

Gwladys stared.

"Do you mean, Tony Rives, that your sister is coming all the way over to Paris to talk to you about *me*?"

"Certainly."

"What does she know about me? Or us, for that matter?"

"Enough."

Gwladys shrugged her shoulders and pretended to be concentrating on her bottle of sun-tan oil.

"I suppose you've been a good boy and written her everything," she said, after a pause. "What is she really like, this wonderful Edith?"

"Ah, now you're asking," I answered, smiling, as I leaned back against the pole of our umbrella. "*Voilà toute une histoire.* Perhaps I could best describe her as a brain with a chain and ball. She sees everything, absolutely everything. But it's as if she saw it all from a prison window."

Gwladys sniffed.

"I suppose she disapproves of you and me being here together."

I threw up my hands.

"Oh, as to that, there's no question!"

"Is she so good herself then?" she asked.

"Irreproachable."

Gwladys sighed.

"Good people can be so hard," she said. "I wonder if they don't cause most of the harm in the world? Is she religious?"

I had to consider this for a moment.

"I should doubt if she's a Christian," I answered. "I should say that she was a pagan. Not a joyful pagan, but a fearful one. Constantly cowering in anticipation of the wrath of murky and unreasonable gods."

"Do these gods watch over her?"

"Not to protect her," I answered easily. "But they check up on her. To see if she is living up to her own exhausting lights."

Gwladys looked up through her dark glasses, over the brightly colored bathing suits, at the sea.

"I'm not sure if I get the picture," she said slowly, "and I'm not sure that I want to. I gather that people do what she tells them to do. But why do they? Is she rich?"

I laughed.

"You've been too long in Europe, Gwladys," I reproached her. "There are other ways of influencing people. Edith is always scandalized if anyone even insinuates that she's got a penny more than her neighbors. Actually, of course, she has a whole sock."

Gwladys shook her head disapprovingly.

"I can't understand people like that," she said. "What I've had, I've always spent, thank God."

"But then you, dear," I said, taking her hand, "are a wicked woman."

Gwladys Kane and I had gone to Venice for the month of August, to sit on the beach at the Lido and to discuss easily and without embarrassment, under a clear Adriatic sky, the arguments for and against our getting married. Gwladys had been twice married and twice divorced; she was a few years over forty and hence a few years older than me. She was very thin and had a pale, bony face with a kind of languid madonnaesque beauty that appealed to me as a critic of painting. Like myself, she had lived abroad for years; she had spent the war in Lisbon and was well known in American expatriate circles. When I first met her in Paris, just after the liberation, she was recovering from the effects of a nervous breakdown. It had left her listless and apathetic, a state of mind which actually intensified her charm to my eyes, though it was considered tiresome in the nervous hurly-burly of her old world. She had lost her taste for society and for the theater and even for love. She wanted only to be left alone in her room at the Ritz, surrounded with flowers, and turn the pages of the books of poetry that she now incessantly read. I used to call on her when she let me do so, for she was pleased to think that I was "different" and that she and I had something to say to each other. This was flattering to me, for I still thought of her as the beauty that she had been in Paris of the early thirties. There was much, perhaps too much, of the observer in my point of view. I loved women like Gwladys at any stage of their development, from the young girl in whose grace and vitality I could feel the germ of a charm that might one day attract the world, to the older and sadder woman in whose facial lines I could read the history of past successes. And then, too, I must confess, I was titillated by the sense of having an affair or rather, of giving the appearance of having it. My love life had not been the most satisfactory chapter of my thirty-nine years, and I had a natural desire to hide this from my friends and to affect the airs of one in the throes of a great passion. Gwladys, on the other hand, was indifferent to these considerations, and when we went to Venice it may have cemented our union in the eyes of other observers, but it did little to contribute to our own greater intimacy. We had reached the point, however, where as between ourselves we no longer worried about the failure of emotion. I was lonely, and Gwladys wanted someone to make hotel reservations and to tip porters. At least, so I told her. She would take me by the hand and look at me sadly with her melancholy eyes and say:

"No, Tony. It's more than that. Quite a bit more."

I always maintained a correspondence with my sister, Edith, and as Gwladys suspected, I had been filling my letters with anecdotes of our life at Venice. I am afraid that I had allowed myself to show off and had managed, as if unintentionally, to give the impression that we were living together. It was only natural, I suppose, that I should have wanted to shock her. Our parents had died when I was a child, and Edith, more than ten years my senior, had brought me up and supplied me with all the frustrations that I might otherwise have escaped. I do not mean this quite as cynically as it sounds. I realize entirely that I needed Edith's love and that she lavished it upon me, even after her own children were born; I realize in fact that she supplied me with that indispensable sense of having somebody who would always love me, not for what she wanted me to be or for what I tried to be, but for what I really was. But even as I realize it, I can still resent my sense of the overwhelming negative that her sad and worried face had cast over the scene of my unenterprising childhood.

"Will she put her foot down?" Gwladys asked. "Will she rant and rave?"

I smiled. It was obvious even to Gwladys that I liked talking about Edith.

"No, she'll be very quiet," I said. "She's devilishly intelligent. That's not her strongest weapon, though. Her pores are what she uses to best effect. She exudes a sort of misty disapproval that paralyzes the will."

Gwladys stared at me in horrified fascination.

"And then, like a snake, she strikes?"

I shrugged my shoulders.

"It's hardly necessary," I answered. "The victim can't move. Sometimes Edith takes pity on him and slips through her own smoke screen to hold his hand."

Gwladys shuddered.

"Why is she like that?" she asked.

"Why indeed?"

"I don't think I'd care to meet her," she continued, rubbing the sun-tan oil on her arms. "I'm glad that I shall be staying on in Venice. While you, like a good boy, go running to your big sister's side. I imagine that I shall find you dangling, when I get to Paris, from the window of her hotel. She'll have strangled you, no doubt, in her apron strings. She or this Diana. Who is Diana, by the way?"

"Edith's niece. Or rather, George's niece."

"A little girl?"

"No. About thirty. And very plain. It's always been a rather tiresome family joke that she's in love with me."

"Ah, well, then," Gwladys said in a tone almost of relief, "you'll be well looked after in Paris. I needn't worry."

But I had no intention of leaving her to the passive immunity of her chosen retreat.

"I trust that doesn't mean," I said severely, "that you have decided to let me down. When I said I'd go up alone to meet Edith, I assumed, of course, that you'd be following."

"Oh, Tony," she protested. "You know I can't bear family scenes."

"The easiest way to avoid one," I continued inexorably, "is by promising to do as I say."

If something was sufficiently in the future it was always possible, eventually, to prevail upon Gwladys. When I bade her good-bye at the hotel late that afternoon she had promised to follow me in two days' time. It had been necessary, of course, for me to do everything in the line of accommodations and planning, but this was always the way with Gwladys, and as I settled back in my comfortable seat by the window on the train, I was able to congratulate myself that things, on the whole, were not working out too badly.

2

The next morning, as my train sped across the long, flat grain fields in the southern vicinity of Paris, my stomach muscles began to tighten at the prospect of my imminent family reunion. I was tingling already with anticipatory indignation at the attitude that I knew Edith and George would take. For had they not always fundamentally disapproved of me? It was fifteen years since I had proudly announced to them both that I had decided to spend my life with pictures rather than dollars. Edith's look of brooding dismay and George's condescending twinkle had solidified me in what may have been only a passing fancy. Even now I can still feel in them what I imagine to be a continued effort to save me from the embarrassment of having to contemplate too closely the ignominy of my choice. I can remember Edith's defense at the time of my making it, so often since repeated to her friends: "You know, Tony's been interested in paintings *all* his life. It isn't as if this were a sudden thing." The disease, she seemed to be saying, had been contracted in infancy. Perhaps I was a fool to interpret them in this fashion. Perhaps they were wonderful, and only queer to me. But as the train turned, and I caught a glimpse in the distance of the Eiffel Tower, I felt a sudden heartwarming reassurance that Paris, after all, was mine and that we were meeting on my territory.

I still think of Edith as many people do of remembered mothers, as tall and Roman and very handsome, and even when I look at her and see how plain she really is, with her unwaved auburn hair, her pale complexion, her long pointed nose and her air of somehow being clad in a dressing gown, I can yet see, in the very dowdiness of the handkerchiefs and loose laces and ribbons that so invariably cling to her, something that smacks of the aristocrat, something perhaps of the integrity of an old and frilled English princess at a charity bazaar. Edith, for all her timidity and caution, has always conveyed the idea of having come through trials and tribulations without even the suspicion of stain or compromise, and behind the deep anxiety in her large gray eyes one had glimpses of a resolution that could never falter. But one might well ask: what trials and tribulations? If Edith was triumphant, over what had she triumphed?

If, in fact, she had had her battles, certainly George, her husband, gave all the appearance of having fought them with her. He was ugly, George, ugly as only very superior beings can be ugly. He had long arms like an ape and walked with a stoop; the top of his head was bald, and his features were bunched together as if he were wincing in pain and being very brave about it. He wore a glittering pince-nez through which his small eyes gleamed humorously, as if to support the questionable validity of the fixed smile that was frozen to his lips. He had, as one might have suspected, a strong series of likes and dislikes to which he adhered with a rigidity of which even one in his profession might be proud. Still more significant, however, than the set quality of his standards was the power with which he was able to convince people that these standards were not personal but absolute. When George, hunching his shoulders so that his head retreated like a turtle's and flashing his eyes to welcome an anticipated compliment, made remarks such as "Of course, *I* never exercise," or "*I* never go to exhibitions of modern art," he produced so uncanny an impression of infallibility that I could only stir uneasily and wonder what it could have been that led me into such deprecated fields. George, without being attractive or handsome or witty, being, indeed, the very reverse of these things, could nonetheless fill me with a sense of confusion and self-doubt by the very firmness of his own self-righteousness and the very blatancy of his affectation of a friendly, homespun tolerance that undermined opposition to his dogma. I used to wonder as a child how Edith could have chosen him, but the answer was simple enough. He accepted the responsibility that she so dreaded, the responsibility for her own decisions. He knew as little of doubt as she of confidence; he was not a judge for nothing. Together they stood against a world that produced wastrels like myself. Their happy home was more than a castle; it was a whole chain of fortifications.

"But I'll never give in!" I exclaimed aloud to myself, suddenly and angrily, and then blushed and stared into my book when I saw how I had startled the two ladies sharing my compartment. It was this fear, I thought miserably, this fear that was always stealing in upon me and making my heart pound so absurdly, this fear that I could never rid myself of, which must have been the very bond that held

Edith and myself together, the fear of emerging suddenly from the shadows into the actual spotlight that the supercilious gods were watching. Edith, I knew, had written poetry as a girl, some of which had even been published in women's magazines. Since her marriage she had never set pen to paper. And are there any so prone to belittle the adventurer as those who have peeked through the open door only to close it on themselves? She had dedicated herself instead to the exposure of what she felt to be the basic insincerity and pretentiousness in people who exploited the color rather than the colorlessness of life. She could spot the insincerity when it was there; I admitted that. She saw it with the clarity of those who have negated color in their own lives. She saw it because she was shrewd and because it *was* there, but she also saw, and perhaps this was the cause of her constant dismay, that it was sometimes accompanied by a spark that dazzled her reluctantly watching eyes and made them turn sorrowfully but full of resolution back to the home that was her primary charge. But, damn it, I almost shouted again to myself, I'll *never* give in! And yet I felt afraid, still afraid, in the very intensity of my excitement.

3

They were staying in an old and respectable hotel where they had a large sitting room filled with the peculiar deadness that the late nineteenth century could give to Louis XV. It was very warm, and they were drinking Perrier water.

"Tony, how nice of you to come!" Edith exclaimed, getting up and embracing me. "My own Tony," she murmured.

George clasped the hand that I reached out to him behind Edith.

"Good to see you, old man," he said, beaming. He looked very well, but then George had never been sick. Edith and I sat down on the sofa, and he hunched himself up on a stiff little chair.

"Have a cocktail, Tony," Edith said heartily. "George, do call the waiter. Let's all have a cocktail. George," she repeated, when he did not immediately rise. He ambled over to the telephone. Edith believed that alcohol had become so necessary to me that it would no longer be a kindness but a cruelty to keep it from me. I daresay she believed this of all expatriates.

"How was the conference in London?" I asked.

"It was fine," she said promptly. "George loved it, and we went to Oxford and Cambridge, too. Austere, but fun."

"Of course, you *like* bad food, Edith."

"I like it more there than I like the black-market food here," she said decisively.

This remark irritated me unreasonably.

"I suppose you haven't come all the way across the Atlantic to criticize me for buying food on the black market," I said sharply.

Edith opened her knitting bag and took out her needle point. She liked to work on this during family discussions, raising and lowering her needle with relentless precision through expanses of floral design.

"We crossed the Atlantic," she said, spreading the pattern on her knee, "for George's conference in London."

"This isn't London," I retorted.

Edith looked up at me calmly.

"Are you so angry with me, Tony," she asked, "for coming to Paris to see my future sister-in-law?"

I got up and walked restlessly to the fireplace, followed by George's twinkling eyes. The apparent reasonableness of my reception was only irritating to me. Whoever took the first step was bound to be in the wrong.

"What it boils down to, I suppose," I answered, "is what your preconceptions are."

"Tony, don't look so serious!" Edith protested. "Aren't you and I going to be able to laugh at things together? The way we always have?"

"Laugh at what?"

She looked away from me.

"You're too prickly," she said. "If there's anything on anybody's conscience, it must be on yours. Certainly neither George nor I have been down to the Lido with a beautiful woman."

I flared up.

"Should that be on my conscience?"

"That's quite a question, isn't it?" George answered for her, smiling with his little smile. "There are those who believe pretty much in sticking to conventional standards until they've been definitively changed. Now, of course, I don't claim to be an authority on morals . . ."

"I'm glad to hear you say so, George," I snapped. "Because I certainly do not regard you as one. So far as I'm concerned, anyway."

George carefully broadened his little smile as he always did whenever he was faced with opposition. His tone became gentler and his twinkle more twinkly as he sensed any falling away in that unanimous assent with which he liked to feel himself surrounded.

"Of course, to some people," he said, "going to the Lido with a beautiful woman might seem the pinnacle of virtuous acts."

"To which group," I said defiantly, "I belong!"

George's smile contracted.

"I never have thought of you as a rake, Tony," he said with a touch of malice. "But some people sow their wild oats later than others. Perhaps it's a case of better late than never."

I turned abruptly from him to Edith in whose face I could read that fear that the things which she was going to say — and no fear on earth would keep her from saying them — might, nonetheless, be the very things that would irrevocably alienate me. And if she did this, would she be fulfilling the trust that she regarded herself, unasked, as having taken over from our late mother?

"I'm sorry, Edith," I said, "but I can't run my life by yours and George's standards."

"You're making a great many assumptions, Tony," she said with dignity. "I think they are all unnecessary. I hope you will introduce me to Mrs. Kane and let us make up our own minds about each other. I'm sure we will manage to find something in common."

"Oh, you'll find something in common, all right," George agreed, winking at me. "You probably each have two arms and two legs. And you undoubtedly each have a tongue."

But Edith had a way of ignoring her husband when she was with me.

"Will I like her, Tony?" she asked.

"Are you willing to?"

"All I know about her is that she's been married twice and divorced twice." Edith's hands moved nervously to her necklace as she spoke. "You can't expect me to be head over heels with enthusiasm on that alone."

I turned from the fireplace and faced her squarely. I felt grimly determined to draw lines and make issues.

"You assume, Edith," I said icily, "that a woman who has had two misfortunes will bring a third on somebody else. You look at her from the pinnacle of your own domestic bliss."

George and she exchanged glances as though they were dealing with a difficult child.

"If you will bring her to see me, Tony," she said patiently, "I won't have to go on making assumptions."

"But will you be fair?"

"Tony, you're too absurd!" Edith retorted. "You expect me to welcome with open arms a divorcée whom I've never even seen!"

"Edith, be careful," I warned her. "You may go too far!"

"Too far!" she exclaimed, getting up. "Who do you think you're talking to? How can I possibly go too far when it's a question of your own good? I have nothing to say about Mrs. Kane except that appearances are against her. And I'm perfectly willing to let her overcome that. But you want too much, Tony. You want my blessing on a blank check. And that most certainly you are not going to get."

George ambled over as if he were trying to get between us.

"As we say in the law," he said with a twinkle, "there's a rebuttable presumption against the lady. But we can be good lawyers. We can rebut."

When Edith took the tone that she was now taking, all my irritation usually vanished, and I would suffer the shame that I had once suffered as a child when I had broken into her closet to bedeck myself in her scarfs and dresses, pretending that I was Cardinal Richelieu, only to be discovered and reprimanded and made to feel what I was, a silly child ludicrously arrayed. But that afternoon in Paris the mood in which I had gone to greet her had a durability unprecedented among the attitudes that I had struck in the past. There were things that I had wanted to say for a lifetime, and now, I knew, they were going to be said. I pulled myself up, draping the imagined scarfs around my shoulders with an air of haughtiness, and became, for a moment, the cardinal.

"I don't give a fig for your presumptions!" I cried in a voice that was unfamiliar even to myself. "Or whether or not you rebut them. I'm through with your everlasting doubts and quibbles. You've neither of you ever approved of me or of any of the people or things I've cared about! You don't like my interest in pictures. You don't like my clothes. You're terrified of anything out of the ordinary. You want to creep through life behind a gray screen. But I repudiate all that! I affirm life!"

To my exasperation Edith simply came over to me and put her hands on my shoulders.

"Do you really mean that, Tony?" she asked. "Can you really look at me and say that?"

"I can," I said with petulance, moving restlessly to escape her grasp. She held me tightly. Then she released me and put a finger on my new red Charvet tie.

"The reason I don't like your clothes, Tony, is only that they're in such poor taste." She ran her finger down over my lapel. "Or do they help you to affirm life?"

I turned away and picked up my hat.

"I think perhaps we've said all that there is to be said on the subject," I said rudely.

"Tony, are you crazy?"

"By your standards I'm worse." And I gave myself the pleasure of slamming the door behind me.

When I got downstairs I was in such a state of nervous

excitement that I had to go into the little bar near the lobby and order a dry Martini. I supervised its mixture carefully, to ensure that the right amount of gin was used. The process, anyway, was soothing, but after the first sip, as I was smacking my lips and making an effort to relax my tightened insides, I heard my name called. It was Diana, and she was hurrying across the room to me.

"Aunt Edith tells me there's been a row," she said with wide-open eyes. "She sent me down to ask you to come back. I was looking up and down the street, and then I spotted you in here. My, I'm glad to see you!"

Diana, as I have said, was my brother-in-law's niece and nearly thirty. She lived with Edith and George, whose children were all married, in a state of semi-dependence. She was large and clumsy and painfully good, almost a caricature of the goddess of her name. She had straight brown hair, shining eyes, and a gushing, exclamatory air that seemed impregnated with a constant, faint perspiration. Her cheeks were round, and her square chin stuck out before them to give her face the determined look of an aggressively concealed timidity, but her big eyes showed all her goodness of heart.

"You're the one member of the family I'm always glad to see, Diana," I said warmly. "But don't try to be the peacemaker. Not this time."

She shook her head firmly.

"I won't."

"You won't?"

"No. This time I'm all on your side. I don't care what Uncle George and Aunt Edith have said about Mrs. Kane. I'm perfectly sure that she's wonderful. I've seen her picture in *The Tatler*."

I felt overcome with gratitude.

"She's even more beautiful than her pictures," I said.

"You can't expect them to understand women like that," Diana continued gravely. "They've led such restricted lives. And they know it, too. They envy you, Tony. That's why Aunt Edith is over here. She doesn't want you to have something that she's never had."

I put down my drink and looked into her round, serious face and wondered that anyone could be so young at thirty. I always felt this when she was naïve enough in her loyalty to articulate my own visceral reactions to any particular situation. For it was my misfortune not to be able to kid myself with absolute success. When a girl like Diana, if I could call her that, a dear sweet girl, let her misguided affection for a trivial fool like myself lead her into the fallacy of oversimplifying a deep and complicated woman like my sister, I could only feel the self-disgust that comes with false leadership.

"Edith doesn't want to lead my life, Diana," I protested. "She simply wants it recorded in the log that she warned me."

"Oh, Tony." Diana shook her head sadly. "She wants much more than that. You think you see through her, and at times you do. But at the last minute you come round." She looked rather frightened at her own temerity. "Forgive me, Tony. But you eat out of her hand. And I'm a fool to tell you that."

It occurred to me that she was. Nothing irritated me more than the insinuation that Edith controlled me. It made me defiantly want to reassert the true nature of our essential intimacy against the world. If Diana had been trying to reconcile us she could hardly have done a better job.

"If I have to eat out of her hand, Diana," I said coolly, "it's nonetheless true that she has to feed me."

4

When Gwladys arrived two days later, I met her at the station and told her about the row.

"But that's wonderful, Tony dear," she said absently, looking helplessly about for a missing bag. "Now I won't have to see her at all. I'm so glad."

I had to look for a porter and get her baggage under control, but as soon as we were alone in the back seat of the cab I returned to the subject.

"I'm not sure that it's quite as simple as that," I pointed out. "I'd hate to think of Edith going blithely back to New York in the full confidence that she has done her duty and that I am beyond recall."

"What earthly difference does it make?" she protested. Then she slipped her arm under mine. "Let's forget all about Edith, Tony. I'm glad I had a chance to be alone in Venice. It gave me time to think about us. And do you know what? I was terribly lonely. I really was."

I glanced somewhat fretfully at the pale, beautiful face beside me.

"No one to order meals?" I retorted. "No one to tip porters?"

"Oh, Tony, don't go on that way," she said, giving my arm an impatient little squeeze. "Let's get married and take a trip to the Indies."

I smiled in spite of myself.

"You'll certainly need somebody if you're planning a

trip," I said. "I'm not sure if it's a husband or a courier. But I shall consider the matter. And in the meanwhile let's give poor Edith one more chance. Let's have dinner with her tonight."

I was surprised at the stiffness of the resistance that I ran into. When Gwladys had said that she had a horror of scenes and that she was morbidly shy, she had been telling no more than the truth. My description of Edith had apparently conjured up in her mind a composite image of every human being in her lifetime who had ever disapproved of her, and she struck out against being subjected to the pain of this meeting with the vehemence of a child who is afraid of the dark. I had not thought there was that much stubbornness in her rather inert personality. I was completely unsuccessful in persuading her to dine with the Macleans that night, but the next day I managed to get her to commit herself to the following evening. When I called Edith she at once, as always, brushed aside any reference to the past.

"But, Tony, don't be a goose. Of course, I don't care about the other day," she said. "I should love to meet Mrs. Kane."

"You'll be nice to her?"

"Tony. You *are* an idiot."

As Gwladys refused point-blank to go to the Macleans' hotel for cocktails it was agreed that I should take her to the restaurant where we were to meet them. Diana was not to be present. The selection of the place and the ordering of the meal George had left to me with the self-deprecation that he loved to assume in matters that he really regarded as beneath his consideration. Gwladys and I, as usual, were late, and the Macleans were already there when we arrived, with an air of having waited for some time. After the first mumbled greetings there was a general retreat behind menus. The dinner was certainly not much fun for anyone except George who, thanks to a liberal dose of cocktails, held forth interminably on the glorious year that he had spent, when a young man, as Justice Holmes' secretary. I busied myself with the dinner, discussed the courses at length with the waiter and showed off outrageously by sending every dish back to the kitchen for a little more of this or a little less of that. Edith would have provided, I suppose, a comic relief to my fussiness in the eyes of a neutral observer. Obsessed with health as I was with taste, she seemed to parody my actions by snatching a plate from her husband on the grounds of indigestibility or pleading with him not drink from the pitcher of water that he had insisted on ordering. Hardly could she talk, so closely did her roving eyes take in the details of our large and meagerly enjoyed meal. The Judge, however, could be cruel, particularly when Edith's preoccupation cut into his monologues.

"My good wife," he said testily to Gwladys, "is as solicitous for my health as she is indifferent to my comfort. I sometimes wonder whether it is concern for my welfare or a morbid preoccupation with the exact fulfillment of her rôle of gastronomic censor."

Gwladys had been watching the bickering between them with eyes that vividly expressed her amazement that such discord could exist among the good. Her sympathy for her own sex, however, was spontaneous and complete, nor was she, to my surprise, too timid to voice it.

"But I think Mrs. Maclean is so right," she said suddenly. "I've never trusted the water here. It's not like what we get at home at all. When I first came over I used to miss Poland water. Do you know Poland water, Mrs. Maclean? My mother used to travel with bottles and bottles of it."

Edith looked at her in surprise.

"From Poland Springs?" she exclaimed. "Why I should think I do! I was practically brought up on it."

"It's so clean and fresh," Gwladys continued nostalgically.

"And pure," Edith added with a little smile that took in, as Edith's smiles always did, the slightly ludicrous aspect of the nostalgic. Yet the door was held open. The door, I supposed, for redemption. "It has a quality entirely of its own," she continued. "Like Maine itself." They were still talking, apparently, about Poland water.

Gwladys seemed to perceive that the door was ajar, for she hurried to squeeze herself through it with a precipitation that amazed me.

"How I should love to be back in Maine!" she exclaimed. "With the seagulls and the sea air and those green, green mountains! Is there anything lovelier in the whole world?"

"Nothing in the world," Edith answered with feeling. "We should all be there now. It's best in the fall."

"You sound like a character in a Henry James novel, Gwladys," I said sourly. "Mourning the lost innocence of your early American childhood."

"Listen to him," Edith retorted. "He just doesn't know, does he? His seagulls are all in the Ritz bar."

Their mutual laugh expressed the sudden spurt of their understanding.

5

Following the unexpected success of this first meeting, the Macleans, Diana, Gwladys, and I embarked on a program of sightseeing to serve as the background for our better acquaintance. George was conscientiously anxious to see everything, and Gwladys, like so many expatriates, was languidly interested at having the unexpected opportunity to examine the unknown sights that had so long surrounded her. It was fun for me, of course, to have so ample a chance to show off to others without serious fear of interruption or criticism. As a veteran tourist I knew everything, from the grilled monogram of a sovereign on a gate to the faded coat of arms of an old-maid princess on a book of prayer. Walking in the garden of Marly and St. Cloud, climbing the horseshoe staircase at Fontainebleau, or seated on a marble bench bordering the *tapis vert* at Versailles looking down at the watery expanse of the canal, I would philosophize, perhaps in greater detail than my audience appreciated, on the significance of Bourbon landscaping, how it represented a projection of the formal garden into the surrounding forests, a defiance of the very force of nature itself.

"Tony never did like nature," Edith said to Gwladys after one of my harangues. "He likes wide stretches of gravel and red and yellow flowers. He was born after his time."

The others laughed with an enthusiasm that put me on notice of the growth of a spirit of defection in our little group. Gwladys, I could see, was entirely intrigued by my sister. She had lived so long in the leisurely, almost stately give and take of cosmopolitan wisecracks, where intellectual laziness bars penetration beyond the *mot juste,* that she found it pleasant to talk with Edith who, despite her emphasis on domesticity, was an extremely intellectual woman and willing to stay with a subject indefinitely once she had started it. Gwladys would timidly bring forth a confession of her fondness for Edith Wharton's novels or for the paintings of Mary Casatt; she would volunteer that she had always longed for the time in which to read or look at pictures, and Edith, amused at what her younger friend chose to regard as the summit of artistic achievement, but tolerant, nonetheless, and full of knowledge of the ladies mentioned, albeit theirs had been territory long traversed, would, without even a hint of superiority, meet Gwladys cheerfully on her own plane and ramble about with her, intellectually, so to speak, arm in arm. If Gwladys had passed the stage of looking down on women like Edith as only dowdy and had reached the point where she trembled in anticipation of their finding her superficial, it was also true that Edith, freed from her sense of evil in the divorced and childless, was now perturbed at the prospect of being crossed off as a distinguished frump. Their mutual relief at finding themselves not so taken for granted resulted, after a short interim of mutual politeness, in the sudden explosion of their recognized congeniality. I soon found myself having to listen incessantly, when alone with either one of them, to her praises of the other. In our daily expeditions I discovered that I was less and less the leader, and I began to feel a bit sour, when in some museum, long familiar to myself, I would be rushing through the more routine rooms, accompanied by the indefatigable Diana, en route to the little-recognized wonder that I was peculiarly qualified to reveal to the others, only to turn and find that Edith and Gwladys, far from being at my heels, would be way in the rear, oblivious of my example, exclaiming over some small painting or snuff box on which their eyes had mutually lighted. I had Diana, it was true, and she hung on my words, making little explosive noises of appreciation at each story that I told. She loved my stories — at least, I believed her when she told me so — but she remembered nothing of them. Her big frame was constantly shaken with the gusty winds of an enthusiasm that passed through it and left no trace of its passage. She was a poor substitute for my lost audience.

I was beginning to be rather bored and impatient with the whole business when it came suddenly to a head one afternoon at Chantilly. It was the first cool day of autumn, and there were leaves on the broad grass around the moat of the château. For once I had got Gwladys away from Edith, and we were leaning on the rail of the little bridge near the main gate, waiting for the others and tossing bread to the carp.

"Do you suppose Edith went back into the château to have another look at the Poussins?" she asked. "She was going to explain to me what it was you saw in them."

My sensation of mysterious female alliance became suddenly intolerable.

"I wouldn't take everything Edith says as gospel," I warned her. "She's very deep, you know."

"Edith?" Gwladys laughed almost condescendingly. "She's the frankest person in the world. Her goodness is right there on top, where you can see it!"

"Don't be too sure about that."

Gwladys turned from the carp and eyed me in her lazy, inquiring way. I thought I could see a hint that she was wondering if I had guessed something.

"You think she has some deep game?" she asked. "Poor Edith. You're so hard on her."

I broke off a big chunk of bread and flung it into the water. It was too big for even the largest carp to swallow, but they surged furiously beneath it, forming with their big sucking mouths a layer between the bread and the surface of the water on which the object of their appetite bounced like a basketball carried over the floor by the striking hands of many players.

"You're very sure of Edith," I retorted. "You have no doubt but that she's all on your side. How can you really think it possible? When you think what she is?"

Gwladys stared at me.

"And what is she?"

I shrugged my shoulders.

"I thought we were agreed," I said, as casually as I could, "that she's a prude."

I knew that I had gone further than I should, but it was too late. I had crossed my Rubicon.

"And a prude would have to disapprove of me?" Gwladys asked in a low tone. "Is that it, Tony?"

"Oh, you know, my dear," I said impatiently. "It's all so obvious, and we've been over it a hundred times before. Edith's standards are absurd but there they are. East shall be East, and West shall be West. What can *I* do about it?"

I tried to avoid the steadiness of her gaze. My eyes followed the gambols of the carp around the retreating piece of bread.

"Why should you *do* anything about it," she asked in a sharper tone, "when you really believe in it? You say we've been over this before. Not this. No, Tony. I knew from the beginning that Edith disapproved of divorce. So do I. All I wanted was a chance to show her my side of the picture, and I got that chance. I think she understands. But you take the position that our differences are irreconcilable. That Edith's principles admit of no exception."

I turned to her, still impatient.

"You can't teach an old dog new tricks."

We exchanged a long look, and I read my full warning in her suddenly determined eyes. I knew Gwladys well enough to know that, although just, she could also be firm. We regarded each other like two nations which reluctantly accept the fact that a seemingly trivial border incident has brought them to the verge of war.

"You say that, Tony," she said gravely, "because it's what you *want* to believe. You don't want Edith to be reconciled."

"Don't be absurd."

She shook her head.

"It's not absurd," she said firmly. "Why it should be true, I don't entirely understand, but what I see, I see now clearly. You can't bear Edith and me being such friends."

"Oh, Gwladys," I protested, "you're making a fuss over nothing! The only thing I mind is the way you both leave me out of things. Now don't go on this way."

She put her arm under mine and led me away from the railing and down the cobblestone drive.

"Listen to me, Tony," she said in her gravest tone. "We don't have to kid ourselves. We had no illusions when we went to Venice. You knew my attitude, and I knew yours. We knew that if it didn't come off there would be no hearts broken. Let's keep it that way. Shall we?"

Certainly nothing that she had said was anything but the absolute truth, but the truth was a luxury that I liked to toy with in moments of egotistical reflection rather than a medicine that I cared to swallow from the end of a sternly extended spoon.

"That may be easier for you than it is for me," I said bitterly.

She pinched my arm.

"That's just what I mean, Tony," she said. "That tone of

yours! That injured tone. It's not honest. You don't really care a fig for me. I wouldn't mind if you'd admit it. But I cannot go on with this dishonesty. This game that you're playing with yourself!"

We were almost back to the car, and I stopped to face her.

"I take it, Gwladys," I said, in a firm, polite tone, "that any tentative plans which you and I may have made should now be regarded as in abeyance. I can only say that I am happy to leave behind with you, if not pleasant memories of myself, at least the delightful prospect of a friendship of increasing intensity with my dear sister."

She looked at me quizzically for a moment and then, quite suddenly, gave me a light peck of a kiss on the cheek.

"Poor Tony," she said softly and got into the back of the car where she opened her guidebook and appeared to be absorbed until the others had come.

6

I have never been as disgusted with life as I was on the drive back to Paris and the subsequent evening in town. I maintained a stubborn silence, refusing even to answer George's tiresome quips and resolutely turning my face from Edith's look of inquiring solicitude. George's mood, as usual, brightened as mine sank, and the general gloom was streaked with the intermittent lightning of his legal jokes and anecdotes. I barely nodded good-bye to Gwladys when we dropped her at her hotel, and when Edith asked me what I planned for the evening I replied savagely that I was going to get drunk. This provoked another story from George about an Irish alcoholic and a county judge. In the middle of it I asked the chauffeur to stop the car and let me out. I had walked half a block before I discovered that Diana was following me breathlessly.

"What do you want?" I asked irritably.

"I want to get drunk too," she said.

"Well, come along then."

We must have gone to five or six different night clubs before we ended up, in the early hours of the morning, drinking champagne in the deserted court of my hotel. We were waited on by an infinitely patient and infinitely disapproving attendant, old enough to have been my father. Yet I was not really drunk. I never got really drunk.

"They've formed a league against me," I told Diana. "My sister and Gwladys. It's an unholy alliance. The Old World with the New. To hell with them!"

Diana nodded vigorously.

"To hell with them!" she echoed loudly.

"Let's drink to a new life," I proposed, "with new freedom! Freedom from George. Freedom from Gwladys and her gay, soulless friends." I put a wonderful emphasis on the word "gay," an irony positively Byronic. "Freedom above all from Edith and her cheerless world. Because none of those worlds exist, Diana! They're only attitudes that have been haunting me since I was a child. Now I'm going to be *me!*"

"To me! I mean, to you!" Diana cried unsteadily and flung her glass into the middle of the large dark court. The shocking sound of its smash brought back the old attendant with an intensified air of disapproval. I began to feel that I was leading Diana astray. Even though, for the first time in our relationship, she was showing a will of her own. She was sitting up very straight, and her face fairly glowed with a triumphant enthusiasm. It seemed to me in the semi-darkness that she had at last taken on the attributes of the divine huntress and might at any moment toss off the restraining fussiness of her lamentable clothes and bound away into the night, beautiful in her strength if not her femininity. I was alone in Paris with an Amazon.

"You mustn't do that again," I warned her. "But I'm glad you did it once. It was beautiful."

"If we get thrown out of here," she said with a toss of her head, "there are other bars."

"But this is my hotel, Diana."

"There are other hotels, then."

Well, of course there were. And I had spent my whole life in only one, or at the most in two. I knew at this point, with a superb clarity, not only that I was jettisoning my experiments of the last fifteen years but that I was going to throw my glove, at long last, in the face of both my worlds. As I looked at Diana's glowing face it seemed to me that I had found a well of uncritical kindness in which I could drown forever my injured ego.

"Diana — " I began. Exact as my memory usually is, I do not pretend to remember the words I used. When I had proposed to her, however, for that is what I assume I had done, she burst into tears. I thought for an awful moment that she was going to revert to the injured schoolgirl. But I misjudged her. She was still an Amazon, if a wounded one. She continued to weep and say nothing.

"I'm sorry the idea is so upsetting," I said with awkward sarcasm. "I know I'm not much of a catch, but I didn't know it was as bad as that."

Diana blew her nose and made a great effort to pull herself together.

"What about Gwladys?" she asked.

"That's all over. What there was of it. Which wasn't, I added after a moment's thought, "anything very much."

"That happened this afternoon?"

I nodded.

"But Tony, isn't this what they call a rebound?"

I looked at her anxious, bulging eyes and suddenly smiled.

"Whatever it is, Diana," I said, "it's yours for what it's worth. You can consider it, as your Uncle George would say in the law, a continuing offer. It can be accepted at any time."

Diana threw back her head and laughed hysterically.

"Oh, Tony, you're so funny!" she cried. "I don't know what to make of you." Then suddenly she was serious. "If you're only rebounding," she continued more timidly, "I'll certainly take you. But if you're doing this because Aunt Edith wants you to — well, that's another thing."

I stared.

"*Does* Edith want me to?" I demanded.

Diana blushed deeply.

"I think she does."

All I could do was laugh helplessly.

"Well, I give up," I said. "Whatever I do, Edith seems to be lurking in the back of the picture. I can't fight it forever. Haven't we drunk to my liberation from Edith?"

Diana's face lighted up again.

"Of course, we have, dear Tony!" she exclaimed. "And we're going to do it again. This time for keeps!"

She seized the bottle of champagne and filled her glass to overflowing.

"To us!" she exclaimed, raising it above her head. "Edith or no Edith! To us, Tony!"

"Diana," I said severely as I watched her drain the glass. "Don't you dare break that glass. Diana!"

But even as I leaned over hurriedly to grab her arm she hurled it triumphantly out into the middle of the court. It struck the statue in the fountain with a loud crash, and we fled like children before the ire of the returning waiter.

7

And so it all happened. When I woke the following morning I had a splitting headache, but otherwise I felt calm and resigned. I was not even tempted to call Diana and treat the whole thing as an alcoholic joke. I knew that it was deadly serious, and I knew that she knew it. I had no desire, either, that it should be otherwise. It was with a proud sense of bearing a message of electric surprise that I presented myself at Edith's door immediately after breakfast and loudly knocked. It opened at once, as if I had been expected, and Edith stepped out to embrace me on the threshold. Behind her stood George, all smiles and twinkles.

"I guess we'll have to check the books," he said, "and see if it's permissible for a man to marry his brother-in-law's niece."

So they knew. I felt a moment's irritation, and then, with a rueful little smile, I resigned myself to the not wholly disagreeable prospect of suffocation in the big hot blanket of family congratulation. For once everyone was on my side, and there were no issues. Even Gwladys called up later in the day to express what seemed to be her unqualified and unsurprised approval. I was oppressed with unanimity, but oppression can be relaxation. I had given up. Just what I had given up was not entirely clear, but I had nonetheless a sense of expiring resentments. I was even able to answer, without snapping, the hundred and one little questions that Edith kept putting to me in an effort to reassure herself that all was for the best. For Edith's sense of instability was far too deep to permit of more than temporary jubilation, and before the evening of the first day the delight had faded from her eyes and she was asking me, "You *are* happy, aren't you?" and "It *is* what you want, isn't it?"

A day or so before I would probably have answered in the negative, regardless of the actual state of my feelings, for the mere satisfaction of seeing the anxiety flood into Edith's eyes. To withhold from her the steady stream of reassurance on which she so depended had in it some of the nervous satisfaction that comes with hiding liquor from an habitual and provoking alcoholic. But it is a satisfaction, after all, immediately followed by remorse and self-disgust. That, I suppose, is what I was giving up when I say I had given up. I had returned to the arms of Edith, if you will, but it was not truly the homecoming of defeat. I was coming of my own free will.

We returned to New York together, Edith and George and Diana and I, where the wedding took place just before Christmas. Diana has proved to be a good wife, and I have been happy. I do not say, as Victorian writers of fiction are apt to say in their concluding paragraphs, that "a gentle arm is on mine as I write" or that "a pair of gentle eyes are looking over my shoulder." As a matter of fact, I intend to make quite sure that Diana never sees these lines. For she has been a good wife, not so much in the ideal sense as in the sense of what I wanted. She has a stubborn will power and gets her own way in most things, but that is the way I like it, particularly as I know that she tries to exercise her will power in my own interests. She is absorbed in my health and happiness and utterly uninterested in my work. She is rather like Edith in this respect; in fact she is rather like a devoted nurse. But she is a dear, and I am devoted to her, and I take great care never to hurt her feelings.

We live in New York and, needless to say, we see a lot of Edith and George. I have often wondered, a bit uneasily, to what extent Edith had planned ahead of time the exact course which events had taken that fall in Paris. We only spoke about it once, and then I got nothing out of her. It was at my wedding reception, in Edith's house, while she and I were standing together in the middle of the big room after the dissolution of the receiving line. I leaned over close to her.

"Edith," I said, "you can tell me now. Now that I'm safely on the hook."

She looked at me furtively from under the enormous brim of her hat. Always lacy, she was unusually so at a wedding. It intensified her air of nervous irresolution.

"Tell you what?"

"Did you plan to get Gwladys away from me and put Diana in her place?" We looked at each other for a startled moment, and my smile became slightly frozen. "Did you know that I'd be left out of your friendship and that Diana would be there to solace me?"

Edith, an incomparable woman, could sometimes smile in the midst of her most brooding moments.

"You must think I have no one to think about but you, Tony," she said. "One of the nicest things about my trip to Paris, aside from your engagement, was my meeting

Gwladys. I plan to see a lot of her this winter when she comes over. After all, there's no friend like a new friend, is there?"

Saying which she turned me around and pushed me gently back to my bride while she went off to greet some decrepit governess of my childhood or some ancient relative of a deceased aunt by marriage. She had inundated the reception with the old and poor and dependent in her terror of leaving out anyone who might have called her a snob. But as Diana had pointed out to me beforehand, she and I did not really care, and if Edith were going to suffer otherwise, why not let her have her way? Why not, indeed? For Edith, in any event, always ended by having it.

THE EDIFICATION OF MARIANNE

There is another way, if you have the courage.
The first I could describe in familiar terms
Because you have seen it, as we all have seen it,
Illustrated, more or less, in lives of those about us.
The second is unknown, and so requires faith —
The kind of faith that issues from despair.
The destination cannot be described;
You will know very little until you get there;
You will journey blind.

—T. S. Eliot, *The Cocktail Party*

THE EDIFICATION OF MARIANNE

MARIANNE's mother left her father when Marianne was a small baby in the early part of the century. She left Marianne, too, fleeing from the coldness of the Tiltons' New York to the sunlight of the Mediterranean, to freedom and to love. It was a decision that even as an old woman, living on the Riviera by Marianne's generosity, she was never to regret. Mr. Tilton divorced her, as publicly as possible, and settled down, in ostentatious simplicity, to devote himself to the raising of his only child. He never married again; he used to say that the woman did not exist who could be a stepmother to Marianne. His own ancient mother and his maiden sister became ladies-in-waiting in the large but lonely court of the child's very special upbringing. They gave her all of their present, and willingly enough, but at the same time they placed upon her slender shoulders the full burden of their hopes and ambitions for the future.

She grew up, as one might have expected from such a concentration, to do everything well. She dressed well; she played games well; she mixed easily with other girls. In every group that she joined and in each school that she attended she proved herself a decorous and adaptable person. She had beautiful blond hair and blue eyes that really sparkled and the whitest skin; her features were small, and they contracted like a little child's when she laughed. It is perhaps obvious to say that she was like a doll, but she was, a wonderful doll of carefully painted wax with unruffled, perennially curled hair, dressed in silk and satin. It was inevitable, of course, that envious people should have tried to classify her as a prig, an automaton, an over-ribboned creature in love with propriety and in love with herself. Her mother, for example, on one of those rare summers when Marianne, traveling abroad with her aunt, had been allowed to call on her, could only read in the brightness of her daughter's smile a concealed aversion to the maternal way of life. But the amazing, the incontrovertible fact was that with Marianne even the envious were obliged to keep rejecting, no matter what their obstinacy, their own oversimplifications. When her father, thinking once to blunt the seeming exuberance of her optimism, took her for a drive on a warm Sunday afternoon through the lower East Side of the city, she looked happily out of the window and cried: "Oh, Daddy, what *fun* to be poor! What *fun!*" And at that time she was no longer a child. She was seventeen.

"Do you think she'll ever develop taste?" he asked his

sister that evening. It was the only thing that he found lacking in his daughter, but to him it was a serious lack. Mr. Tilton was a cool, thin, grim gentleman who belonged to many clubs that he never used and whose own taste, however good, was wholly intellectual.

"Taste?" Miss Tilton came of a generation where such things were left to men. Behind the lace and the velvet her sentiment, still vibrant, was beginning to stale. "She's always dressed very nicely, I think. I don't know what you have to complain of."

"I don't mean taste in dress, Emily," he said testily. He was always surprised afresh at the magnitude of her fatuity. " I mean taste in people and in pleasures. I know we all love her simple ways, but I confess I'd like to feel that I was more highly regarded than the chauffeur. Do you remember 'My Last Duchess'? 'She liked what'er she looked on, but her looks went everywhere.'?"

"You mean she makes eyes at men?" Miss Tilton asked, shocked.

Her brother closed his lips tightly. He always tried not to be impatient with her.

"No, Emily," he answered drily. "I do not. Although, since you bring the matter up, one does hear that women who are lightly inclined may have generous hearts. Undiscriminating hearts," he added with emphasis.

Miss Tilton was dismayed by her brother's observation, and she considered the matter carefully. There *was* something, after all, that she did not understand in Marianne, something that lurked behind the façade of her brilliant smile, behind the immediate sympathy in her eyes, the light touch of her hand on one's arm, the laugh that seemed to vibrate with spontaneous congeniality, to shut out those who loved her. She was like the beautiful garden in *Alice in Wonderland* that had one tiny, closed gate.

She gives us everything, poor child, Miss Tilton reflected. Must we pry into the one little corner that she reserves for herself?

2

What troubled Mr. Tilton in his daughter was not really, if he had only known it, a very complicated matter. It was simply that she did not believe in anything. In anything at all. Whatever bone or muscle or soul it was in other people that enabled them to love their friends and hate their enemies, to believe in the precepts of God and fashion, to work for their better reward and security and to gaze with satisfaction upon their own accomplishments, this she did not have. If Marianne had no prejudices, neither had she any real enthusiasms. She knew this herself; she had always been aware of the disharmony between herself and others, and it troubled her deeply. For she had no wish to be different or to disappoint people who cared for her. If they wanted her to enjoy parties and dresses and young men, she wanted to put on as good a show as she possibly could. But it was hard to know what she was meant to like and what to dislike. She was like a foreigner traveling in a land whose tongue she has learned but whose words have not yet become the symbols of her own thinking. Life was a difficult game with difficult rules, but they *could* be learned. If she stayed with her aunt and followed her precepts.

"You do things well, my dear," Aunt Emily would tell her. "Too well. You must learn to relax."

It was difficult, however, to relax about marriage, and

everything in Marianne's upbringing pointed to an early and splendid match. She accepted the idea as she accepted everything from the older generation, but she found her usual trouble in adjusting her different assumed attitudes to the varying moods of her family and friends. If she was serious in discussing with her aunt, for example, the virtues of a young man who had been attentive, she would be met with smiles and jokes. Then, it seemed, she had been too "grave." Yet if, on the other hand, she appeared to take the matter lightly, if she joked about love and lovers, she was sternly told that marriage was a serious affair and her "happiness," a sober concept, not a thing to be trifled with. Everything in life, it seemed, had this confused dual nature. One could be gay, but not too gay, and kind but not too kind. One had to care about clothes, but not too much, and the arts, but not too much, and sex, but not too much, and God, but not too much.

"Clarence Lipton must be a very fine young man," she told her aunt one morning after a dance. "He talks about happiness the way you talk about having the house cleaned when we go abroad. As something that people *must* have time for."

The young man of whom she spoke was highly favored by her father. He had no family background, in the Tilton sense of the word, and he was twelve years older than Marianne, but he was nonetheless very young indeed to have reached the position that he occupied in the world of investment banking. Mr. Tilton had checked among his Wall Street friends and had discovered that Clarence was likely to make a fortune. He had all the naïveté, too, that often accompanies the self-made into their success; he gave the appearance, with his fine, strong eyes, his big jaw and square build, of taking the non-business world at its face value, but of being able, nonetheless, to handle it, should it turn out to be something different. Like many who have matured young, he had a reluctantly cynical nature. Underneath he yearned for a world of less complicated premises. He had fallen in love with Marianne, whom he had met on a vacation in the Adirondacks, and courted her heavily, with never failing flowers and long serious speeches.

One night when Clarence had taken her home after a party she found her father still up. He was in the library, sitting alone with a book, and he looked up when she came in.

"Tell me, my dear," he asked her, "do you like young Lipton?"

"Oh, yes, Daddy. I like him extremely!"

He looked at her critically.

"I rather gather from what he said to me this afternoon that he is not exactly averse to you."

She smiled at him, brightly.

"But that's good, Daddy! Isn't it?"

"Why is it 'good'?"

"Well—" She hesitated. "Don't you perhaps want me to marry him?"

He shook his head and looked away from her into the fire.

"My child, it doesn't matter what I want," he said gravely, and he meant it, too, as he said it. "It's what *you* want that counts."

She nodded, embarrassed.

"What do you really think of him?" he pursued.

Again she hesitated.

"Well, what other people do, I guess," she said timidly.

"He's good-looking, and he works terribly hard, and everyone says he's going to be rich — "

"Marianne!" His eyes were on her now, sharp and stern. "How can you be so vulgar?"

"Is that vulgar, Daddy?"

"Of course, it's vulgar. Don't be a child. Do you want to marry for money?"

The tears started into her eyes.

"I only want to do the right thing, Daddy," she protested.

Mr. Tilton gave it up. He told Clarence, however, that he approved, for Clarence, not knowing what customs were, thought that in New York one still had to ask for a father's permission. That evening the happy suitor took Marianne out to dinner, and in his own rather ponderous but entirely coherent manner he asked her to marry him. She accepted, as she thought, with just the right combination of enthusiasm and bashfulness. His face brightened for a moment, but only for a moment. Then the air of gravity returned.

"Do you think you'll be able to care for me always?" he asked, taking her hand. "It's a tremendous step that we're taking, you know. A happy marriage is the most beautiful thing in the world, but it doesn't just happen. It's a serious business. A very serious business, Marianne."

She nodded quickly.

"I know."

"Are you as happy as I am, darling?" he asked. "No, you couldn't be. But I'll try to make you. I'll spend my life trying. That's what love is, you know. Trying to make the other person as happy as you are yourself."

Even more than other people, she noticed, he had the craving to generalize. He could not allow one lonely particular to wander across his path; he had to rush after it and grab it and push it into the brimming basket of his classifications.

"I will try, Clarence," she said simply. "I really will."

At the engagement party a dispassionate Mr. Tilton watched his daughter and her fiancé receive the congratulations of their excited friends. Aware of his remoteness from the general enthusiasm, his sister approached him.

"Don't they look lovely?" she murmured. "And doesn't she look happy, our sweet?"

He glanced at her impatiently.

"I know you don't feel that a father has any right to perception, Emily," he said. "But that is not a matter on which we have ever agreed."

"Oh, Henry!" she protested. "Is that *all* you have to say? On this day of days?"

"We once discussed a certain poem of Browning's, Emily," he said coolly. "Fortunately our Clarence does not read. There is another very pertinent line. 'She ranked her husband's gift of a nine-hundred-year-old name with anybody's gift.'"

Miss Tilton looked bewildered.

"But Clarence doesn't have an old name," she protested. "Far from it," she added with a sniff.

Mr. Tilton turned away from her, resolving, for perhaps the thousandth time, that he would not again discuss the peculiarities of his so highly individual daughter.

3

Mr. Tilton did not live to see how the marriage worked out. He died three months after the wedding, and Miss Tilton took up her residence with Marianne and Clarence.

Clarence was already aware that the presence of another person in his home would not affect his marital relationship. Not that he was dissatisfied with it. Marianne, he repeatedly told himself, was a perfect wife; she was always cheerful and always efficient, and if there was an impersonality in her attitude towards himself and a certain passivity in her lovemaking, well, that, after all, he had to suppose, was the way wives *were*. He was a man, fortunately, who was primarily married to his work and his ambitions. Three sons were born in three years, and, all things considered, he had little enough to complain about. Miss Tilton, despite an increase in petulance as time went by, nodded approvingly to herself when she saw the way her niece looked down the long dinner table, over the gleam of silver and glass, at her handsome husband. The most unobservant of guests could see that there was a sympathy between them. But there always *were* guests. Even Miss Tilton could see that.

Marianne herself found married life easier and more peaceful than she had expected. Clarence had to be away a great deal, and she was able to spend most of her time on their farm in Connecticut which she loved. She had discovered a summer camp near it for children whose parents were employed in a factory in Hoboken that was controlled by Clarence's firm. She used to drive over there during the summer months to help the counselors with their classes and field trips. It was a world that she understood. The aim of the institution was simple, and the values uncomplicated. She could see what she was doing and she had a sense, unique for her, that it was worth while. When she tried to interest her own boys in it, however, they scorned the idea. All three of them took after Clarence.

"If that sort of work interests you, darling," Clarence told her firmly, "go ahead with it. It's fine. I'll see to it that you can run a camp for every business we buy. But remember. It's a woman's work, and the boys *aren't* interested."

Her activities, however, were viewed with the greatest interest by Ardsley Hobart, the director of the camp, a handsome and blond bachelor in his early thirties whose expression wore some of the blandness and serenity so often associated with the professional social worker. Yet behind the serenity one could read, if one had more knowledge of such things than Marianne, an air of almost furtive preoccupation. For Ardsley himself was far from being a serene or contented person. He had a whole future to forget. As an undergraduate at Yale his work on a college paper had attracted attention beyond the limits of the campus; his good looks, his idealism and his disarming willingness to talk on equal terms with men high in business and public life had gained him a position as one of the spokesmen for his generation. Graduating, his choice had seemed infinite, but so, unfortunately, had been his selections. For ten years he had led the life of the organizer, with fellowships and secretaryships, with small, liberal magazines and large youth congresses, with treatises on pacifism and moral rearmament, with big subscription dinners in big hotels. His less sympathetic friends had said that he was marking time until he was old enough for the White House. When he was thirty he suddenly realized that he had ceased to be a spokesman; he had the bitterness of hearing about futures other than his own. He drank steadily for two years and suffered a prolonged nervous breakdown. Since then he had been satisfied with the mild obscurity of the social worker in summer camps and boys' clubs. It was an obscurity, at least, that seemed to have neither past nor future, and its present was soothing and gray.

THE EDIFICATION OF MARIANNE

Into the lethargy of his existence the apparition of Marianne had burst with an impact that was not entirely agreeable. He had been prepared for another idle and interfering patroness, and he had looked forward to the feeding of his own cynicism that would result from the inevitable falling away of her interest. During her visits, however, he was attention itself; he wanted to be sure, for his own embittered satisfaction, that she would have no excuse in his conduct for her ultimate boredom. When he recognized that she was truly unique, that she could help without interfering and advise without patronizing, he was at first disappointed. But this did not last. It could not last with Marianne. The very intensity of her concern made him ashamed of his own inertia. He gave up the movies in the evening and sat with his back to a tree while she read aloud to the girls.

"You're like a good character in a Charlotte Brontë novel, Marianne," he told her one evening as he took her back to her car. "You should have your hair parted in the middle and braided."

"You think I'm too flamboyant?" She laughed as she said this. It occurred to him that it was a silly laugh. But its silliness, in some inexplicable fashion was not a part of her.

"No, it's not that," he assured her, and the silliness, to his own irritation, had now become part of him. "You're quite perfect. Our guardian angel. Where should we be without you?"

"Much better off, I suspect," she said self-consciously. And there was again that laugh.

It was after this that he realized that their mutual interest, or rather her interest, in the camp would not be enough for him. It was clear, however, that it might well be enough for her. Yet could it be, he would ask himself at night, as he lay smoking in his cabin, looking out of the open door to the lake, that a creature so beautiful had been sent to his lonely retreat only to pass him by? To take her satisfaction in things where he found only emptiness? For if he failed to imprint his ego on the smiling surface of what seemed to be her infinite goodness, how else was he to be saved?

Their conversations were almost entirely about the camp, and he felt increasingly hypocritical as he continued to pretend, and pretend successfully, that his interest was as great as hers. One night when he was driving her home he allowed himself, in accordance with a plan, to speak for the first time in derogatory fashion of the way of the welfarer.

"But, Ardsley," she said in surprise. "Don't you *like* the camp?"

"Oh, of course, I like it," he said carelessly. "After all, this sort of thing is my life. But you can't like a thing all the time, can you? Even if it's your life?"

"I think I can," she said slowly.

"You mean you can like the camp *all* the time?"

"I think so. Why not?"

"Can you like all the counselors, too?" he protested, and then paused with a feeling of guilt. "Oh, I know they're good and fine, but don't you ever feel that there's something — well — flabby or inert about them? Don't you ever yearn for someone who will be more biting? More incisive?"

"Oh, no," she said quickly. "I've had people like that in my life. I know *them*."

He felt frustrated and impatient.

"You mean," he continued, "that you never get exasperated with that dietician who's always rubbing her hands and saying, 'Mrs. Lipton, this,' and 'Mrs. Lipton that'?"

"As a matter of fact I've asked her to call me Marianne."

He stared at her in amazement. It had never occurred to him that anyone else on the staff could be on such a basis with her.

"Did you really?" he demanded. "She must have swooned!"

"Do you think the people at the camp are any different from other people, Ardsley?" she asked gravely. "Maybe they are. But I can't see it. I imagine I'm different, too. No, really," she protested when he smiled.

"Do you ever see anything different in *anyone?*" he asked.

"Oh, yes, I suppose."

"Do you ever see anything different in *me?*"

She looked at him brightly, as though they were starting a game.

"What would you like me to see?" she asked.

But it was far from a game to him. He felt suddenly that he could not live for another minute without being distinguished in some way by the wide, serious, innocent eyes before him.

"I'd like you to see in me somebody whom you've brought back to life," he said recklessly. He knew that he was not being honest and that his tone was not honest, but he didn't care. The honesty was in his desire to reach her. "Someone who's risen from the dead. I was nothing, Marianne, before you came here. You were too kind to see that. And now look at me! I can *breathe!*"

"And I did that?"

"You did that."

She shook her head, embarrassed.

"I think you must be exaggerating," she said.

"There's much more that I could say, Marianne," he continued, "if you'd only let me."

"Oh, no!" She put her hand up. "Dear me, Ardsley. That would never do."

And then, very firmly, she directed the conversation back to the camp.

This conversation, nonetheless, put their friendship on a more intimate basis. He became as constant a caller at the farm as she at the camp, and they had long conversations by the pool about the difficulties of being understood in a world that was preoccupied with standard reactions. He nursed the constant hope, only moderately concealed, that their rather misty and sentimental relationship would at last develop into something more vital. Marianne, too, allowed herself to consider this. She had heard that such relationships usually ended in love, and she had heard, too, that the joys of illicit love were the sweetest of all. Once again she saw the dread possibility looming, of having to choose without a criterion. She remembered that some of her friends felt that one owed a duty to love that overrode convention. Yet such things were almost bound to explode into the harsh words and repudiations that so inevitably and unaccountably accompanied the simplest human steps or missteps. This, at least, she knew, was to be avoided. No matter how agreeable it was to listen to the confidences of a person as friendly as Ardsley, as undemanding as Ardsley, as idealistic, as backsliding. And as dependent on her. Why could things never be allowed to remain that way? Why could people *never* let her be?

4

But that was the thing about Marianne. People never would. Aunt Emily watched the comings and goings of the camp director with the satisfaction of an atheist who finds a crack in a graven image. Living with Marianne she had become increasingly fretful at her niece's seeming failure to appreciate the blessings that had been heaped in her lap. Such unworldliness was an implied reproach to those, who, like Aunt Emily, not only cared but envied. When she watched her with Ardsley she decided that her niece was, after all, human, and she smiled to herself. She liked Ardsley, and, of course, she adored Marianne, and she was absolutely sure that nothing was *really* going on, but she could not resist making oblique references to Clarence when he came for the weekend.

"What are you trying to tell me, Aunt Emily?" he asked her one Sunday with a smile. "That Marianne's fallen for this guy?"

"Oh, you men," she said shaking her head. "How you leap to conclusions! There's no keeping up with you. All I'm trying to say is that he's crazy about *her*."

Clarence was suddenly furious. He remembered now that his wife and Ardsley both came from the same small Manhattan group which had never really accepted him, and his eyes narrowed. Had she not always been remote, indifferent even to the heat of his own advances?

Aunt Emily looked at him in alarm.

"Now, Clarence, don't do anything rash!" she exclaimed.

He went to Ardsley that afternoon and ordered him to resign from the camp. He made it brutally clear that he would ruin him if he ever saw Marianne again. To the unhappy lover this treatment had the desired effect. He came to his senses, blinked for a moment at his terrifying rival and hurried off to New York.

That same evening, before dinner, Clarence told his wife what he had done. They were sitting alone on the flagstoned terrace, dressed and drinking cocktails. She stared in perplexity at his angry eyes and watched his fingers turning his glass round and round.

"But why, Clarence?" she demanded. *"Why?"*

"I suppose it's fussy of me," he answered with heavy sarcasm, "to object to my wife's name being bandied about the countryside. To be the joke of every bar."

She looked across the field to the blue hill.

"It was nothing," she said.

"Nothing!" he almost shouted. "I suppose adultery would be nothing either! Perhaps nothing in the world *you* come from. I daresay. But in my world, Mrs. Lipton, and you still *are* Mrs. Lipton, I'll thank you to remember, it's very important indeed."

She noticed with surprise that he really seemed to care. It was more than a question, then, of going through the motions of the little game of husband and wife that they had been playing so long. It was a question after all, of those angry shouts and repudiations. She felt suddenly tired, inadequate.

"I have told you, Clarence," she said. "It was nothing."

"You're like your mother, after all," he said spitefully. "You have no moral sense."

She shook her head at his denseness. It was beyond everything how he could drag in the poor mother she had hardly known. And then, as she was thinking how queer it all was, something gave way inside of her. It was as if she had lost her balance and fallen, very hard, to the floor. She was dizzy for a minute, and then, as she focused her eyes on Clarence's now alarmed face, she felt the spell pass. She leaned back in her chair and breathed deeply. Then she smiled at him, as if he, too, must be glad.

"Are you all right?" he asked.

"I'm quite all right," she said in a low voice. "I'm fine, thank you." There was a long pause during which her thoughts came very fast and clearly. "I've simply decided not to go on being a fool," she continued. "It's as simple as that. You can believe what you want about Ardsley. As for me, you must forgive me, but I will never again discuss this distasteful subject."

She stood up.

"Marianne!" he protested. "Wait a minute! I've been excited, and I'm sorry. If there was really nothing between you . . ."

"I'm through with the subject, Clarence," she interrupted. "I meant that. I really did."

She turned away to the house.

"Marianne!" he called after her. "I'll divorce you!"

She paused for a moment, but only for a moment.

"You may do anything in the world you please, Clarence," she said. "It's a world, I suppose, that belongs pretty much to you. I shall abide by your decision, whatever it is. But I shall not again be a fool. I am through with that. Forever."

5

Marianne did not suffer from her disillusionment. There was, on the contrary, a strange exhilaration in being freed, after a lifetime of effort, from the task of trying to comprehend and live by the standards of others. What they enjoyed was, after all, not her concern; what they believed could only be *their* consolation. It might be good or it might be bad; the important thing was its irrelevance. The morning after her argument with Clarence she went early to the camp and worked until after prayers that night. She reorganized as she had long wanted, the schedule to reflect the suggestions of the National Organization of Summer Camp activities; she interviewed four children who had had bad news from home, and she arranged leave for a counselor whose mother was ill. When she got home that night she was not even interested in Clarence's decision.

He called to her from his study when he heard her step on the stairway. She turned and looked down at him.

"Marianne," he said. "Is it always to be this way between us?"

"You don't understand, Clarence," she said. "I haven't changed. I've grown up. That's all. I can't be Peter Pan forever."

"What will you do?" he asked.

"*Do?* I shan't do anything."

"You make it very hard for me," he said bitterly and turned away.

But that, after all, was his problem. He could make his own classifications and put his own tags on things. He was well equipped for it.

"Good night, Clarence," she said with decision.

The last thing, of course, that he wanted was a divorce. He wanted her to tell him that there had been nothing between her and Ardsley, as he was beginning to believe, but when, as time went on, and she continued adamant in her refusal to discuss the matter, he came to accept the situation. There was even something like relief in the new quiet of their reserved and peaceful relationship. All of Marianne's energy was now loosed upon the camp. The Connecticut camp, of course, was only the beginning. She organized other camps for the children of employees of other businesses in which Clarence had a controlling interest. From these she broadened her field to promote summer camps in general. Clarence, a good businessman, gave her money for her projects in exact proportion to the increase of her fame. Within a few years after their quarrel she had become a well-known figure in the world of social welfare; her influence had spread from children's recreation to hospitals, from hospitals to slum clearance, and finally, as the war started in Europe, to displaced persons. Clarence appeared with her at the speakers' table at subscription dinners, and, little by little, a new congeniality was established between them. There were, as might have been suspected, other women in his life, but such things were not discussed.

"You said you'd never be a fool again, Marianne," he told her one night as they left the Waldorf. "And you've certainly lived up to it. Your father would have been proud of you."

"Daddy?" she laughed, but there was no bitterness in her laugh. "He'd have hung his head in shame. The way the boys do at school. But what can I do?"

Marianne knew that she was criticized for not paying more attention to her sons. Clarence's friends were never tired of pointing out that charity begins at home. Yet she was as good a mother as the boys allowed her to be. Had she been always at home, things would have been no different. They had never, it seemed, really needed her. They were highly independent young men, and like Clarence they were successful at everything they undertook. She tried to understand their rather brutal jokes and their quick absorption of the mores of private-school life; she went up to watch them play football and she entertained their friends, but it was a family cliché that she didn't understand what "it was all about." Her simplest comments were usually greeted with the bray: "Oh, *Mother!*" They liked her well enough; they tolerated her, but it was their father to whom they turned in trouble, and Marianne was not the person to pretend a resentment that she did not feel. She had found her way, and there could be no going back to the strange world of other peoples' facts and other peoples' fancies. It had been a struggle of too many nervous years to permit of compromise now. Time, that had once crawled for her, now sped smoothly by.

6

When Ardsley read of Clarence's death in the headlines of his morning paper, during the first winter after the war, he felt a reawakening of his old curiosity about Marianne. Everything that had passed, or rather that had not passed between them, was well in the past, and he had recovered from the violent and baffling emotion that had held him to her. He had not, however, married, nor had he made much progress in his career, and it was impossible for him not to be aware of the size of the fortune that Clarence's untimely heart attack might have placed in her control. He wrote her a long and, as he considered, moving letter and received a simple note in answer, with a clear and rather touching eulogy of her husband's character. When he called at the house in Sutton Place he found that she had gone to the country for a month. He chatted for a few minutes with the rather mournful butler.

"She won't be coming back here, sir," he said. "She's giving the house to some university. For a research project." He shook his head. "She always said it was too big for her."

It was obvious that she had no lack of plans for her newfound liberty. He did not see her until her return to the city and then only at a large charitable affair in the ballroom of a big hotel. He had been given a ticket by Irene Manners for her table; Irene had recently become chairman of the board of the settlement house that employed him and had proved herself an efficient but exacting patroness. He had attended, however, only partly in fear of Irene. He had also seen Marianne's name among the listed speakers.

He detested such affairs, crowded and noisy, with the same bad food and the same rude waiters and the same difficulty of getting a cocktail, and he kept his eyes on the raised speakers' table and chewed impatiently on his roll. At last they came in, the inevitable guests of honor, the Mayor, the Cardinal, the Admiral and the General, the head of the hospital, the United Nations delegate, the Judge, the Senator. And Marianne. People different from other people by having dined so often on banquet food, waiting for the tinkle of silver on the coffee cups as their signal to rise and speak. And then the applause. The seas of applause. She was dressed, of course, in black, and she seemed thinner and bigger than before. There were circles under her eyes, but they were becoming to her. Her doll-like charm had turned with middle age into a kind of gauntness, a clear and rather noble gauntness. She was statuesque, he reflected at first. She was sexless, he reflected, a moment later.

"I'm so glad Marianne Lipton is speaking," Irene said to him. "She never lets one down. She's always more fatuous than she was the time before."

"I'm surprised she'd speak so soon after his death."

"Oh, Ardsley!" she reproached him. "Don't you know women? Widow's weeds and noble causes and carrying on? Why, she's having the time of her life!"

He laughed.

"But you've never liked her, Irene."

She shrugged her shoulders.

"One doesn't dislike Marianne," she said. "It's not that. One simply finds her a fool. A perfectly amiable, but quite provoking fool. I'm glad that Clarence had the sense to tie up her share of his estate in trust. He didn't want everything he'd earned to go to Hottentots."

Marianne was the first speaker of the evening. She discussed the organization that was collecting clothes for European children and the details of the forthcoming drive. She spoke smoothly and with the assurance that comes from constant speaking; she gave the same emphasis to each sentence and paused without embarrassment during the occasional rounds of applause. There was nothing in the speech, with the exception of the organization details, that was not entirely trite: she spoke of the devastation of the war, the need for children to have strong bodies if they were to have strong minds, the impossibility of peace with hate and the great obligations of America. Ardsley took in the impressiveness of the gathering and wondered how she dared to harangue them with such clichés. Yet, mysteriously enough, they seemed to be with her. It was impossible, he decided irritably, to exaggerate the gullibility of the commercially successful.

"And it will not only be the children of Europe who will benefit," she was concluding now. "I like to think that all the children in our great country who join in this drive, each by giving a coat or a hat or even an old pair of trousers, will themselves benefit from an act that may give them a larger sense of our human family and a less local sense of what the word 'need' can mean. Let us not call it generosity. Let us call it, rather, *our* sense of world citizenship."

She sat down, but she had to rise several times to acknowledge the strong and continued burst of applause. She smiled and nodded; she waved a hand to the crowd, and Ardsley noticed that when the flash bulbs popped, almost in her face, she barely blinked. It was as though she floated over such wide benignant seas, cloaked in the mist of such constant approval and idealism, orating so interminably of causes and improvements and donations, that nothing could trouble her, nothing bring her down to the level of individual criticism that he now so strongly felt himself to represent.

When the speeches were over he accompanied Irene upstairs to a smaller room where a reception was being held for the guests of honor. He found Marianne and took her aside.

"It was so dear of you to write me," she said. "I loved your letter."

"You must have had many."

She shook her head.

"Not as many as all that," she said. "You'd be surprised. My life is different now, Ardsley. I'm on my own, you see." In the silence that ensued she seemed to have nothing to say. Almost nervously, at last, she continued: "Perhaps you would like to come down to the country next week, for Thanksgiving? It'll be the last Thanksgiving there. I'm closing the place."

"But you've closed the house in town, Marianne!"

"Oh, you know that? Yes. I'm closing everything." She smiled. "I don't want to be cluttered up with things."

He reverted to her invitation.

"Won't you be full up with family over Thanksgiving?"

"The boys? No. They're all away at school or college. I tell you, I'm quite alone these days."

He looked at her quizzically for a moment.

"I suppose life always ends by giving us what we've asked for," he said.

"Meaning that I've asked for loneliness?" she answered, smiling.

He retreated before her directness.

"Not that," he said. "But you're dedicated, aren't you, to mankind? You have no time for us."

She still smiled.

"For *us?*" she asked.

"I mean for anyone," he said impatiently. "For friends. You deal in wholesale. There are no individuals in your life." He gathered courage as he spoke. "There never were, were there?"

"No friends?" She laughed, as at the very absurdity of it. "Well, thank heavens, Ardsley, I haven't lost my ability to make friends. I make them every day. One of the reasons I was hoping you could come for Thanksgiving was that I'm having a new friend to stay. Marion Klotz. She's a most interesting person and has had a really fascinating life. She's going to Europe on this clothes mission . . ."

He listened, as his indignation rose almost to fury, while she described the biography and future of Miss Klotz.

"Have it your way, Marianne," he retorted with a pique that, angry as he was, he knew to be childish. "And I hope that you and Miss Klotz will have a delightful Thanksgiving. Give thanks for me that there are so many like you. There's still hope for the world, I guess."

He turned from her astonished expression and made his way towards the door. As he was striding across the lobby, however, he saw an old woman, in black velvet and lace, sitting alone at a table. He was about to pass by when he recognized her as Marianne's aunt, Miss Tilton, whom he had known so well during his visits to the Liptons in the past. Her eyes opened very wide when she saw him.

"Have you seen Marianne?" she asked excitedly, half rising. "She'll be so delighted to see you again, Mr. Hobart!"

"That's what I had hoped," he said. He shook her hand and sat down. "But she isn't," he continued bitterly. "I don't exist for her any more. I never did. She has no use for the sane or the healthy or the independent. Even for you, Miss Tilton."

"Oh, me!" Here the old lady giggled rather meanly. "I hope she loves somebody more than she loves *me*. I just don't count, you know."

It was not agreeable for him to recognize his own reaction in her.

"Yet I bet she does everything for you," he said.

"Oh, yes," she agreed reluctantly. "Everything. She does everything for me. I'm not complaining, mind you."

"And nothing for herself," he continued, forcing himself to face her incontestable virtues. "All she wanted out of life was the love of little people. And I suppose she has got it. But don't you think, Miss Tilton," he said with a return of his reckless irritation, "that she would have found more satisfaction in the arms of a man whom she loved?"

Miss Tilton looked at him with some of the glee that the very old and conservative may feel when face to face with the appallingly indiscreet. She cackled aloud and then suddenly subsided. Her eyes moved over to where Marianne was standing in the corner with a sudden mixture of reluctant awe and hostility.

"No, you're wrong, Mr. Hobart!" she exclaimed with intensity. "You're wrong! Because I know what she is, that girl. You can't have lived with her as long as I have and not know it, God forgive me!"

He stared.

"What is she, then?"

Miss Tilton's drawn, wrinkled face was filled with the burden of her news.

"She's a saint!" she cried. "That is what saints are!"

There was a pause while they faced each other in sudden, inexplicable dismay.

"Is *that* what saints are?" he demanded.

"Of course, it's what they are," she insisted, as if she had to convince herself. "Isn't that why we resent her? Why everyone has always resented her?"

There were things, too many things that he could have said to this. He looked at the almost hysterical old lady for a long moment and then back at Marianne, where she was talking across the room. She saw that he was with her aunt and waved at him, very nicely. He sighed, feeling beaten and inadequate, and got up at last to leave the party.

GREG'S PEG

*And so, upon this wise I prayed, —
Great Spirit, give to me
A heaven not so large as yours,
But large enough for me.*

—Emily Dickinson

GREG'S PEG

It was in the autumn of 1936 that I first met Gregory Bakewell, and the only reason that I met him then was that he and his mother were, besides myself and a handful of others, the only members of the summer colony at Anchor Harbor who had stayed past the middle of September. To the Bakewells it was a period of hard necessity; they had to sit out the bleak, lonely Maine September and October before they could return, with any sort of comfort, to the Florida home where they wintered. To me, on the other hand, these two months were the only endurable part of Anchor Harbor's season, and I had lingered all that summer in Massachusetts, at the small boarding school of which I was headmaster, until I knew that I would find the peninsula as deserted as I required. I had no worries that year about the opening of school, for I was on a sabbatical leave, long postponed, and free to do as I chose. Not, indeed, that I was in a mood to do much. I had lost my wife the year before, and for many months it had seemed to me that life was over, in early middle age. I had retreated rigidly and faithfully to an isolated routine. I had taught my courses and kept to myself, as much as a headmaster can, editing and re-editing what was to be the final, memorial volume of her poetry. But during that summer I had begun to look up from the blue notepaper on which she had written the small stanzas of her garden verse to find myself gazing out the window towards the campus with a blank steadiness that could only have been symptomatic, I feared, of the heresy of boredom. And thus it was with something of a sense of guilt and a little, perhaps, in that mood of nostalgic self-pity that makes one try to recapture the melancholy of remembered sorrow, that I traveled up to Anchor Harbor in the fall.

My wife and I had spent our summers there in the past, not, as one of her obituary notices had floridly put it, "away from the summer resort in a forest camp, nestled in that corner of the peninsula frequented by the literary," but in the large rambling pile of shingle, full of pointless rooms and wicker furniture, that belonged to my mother-in-law and that stood on the top of a forest-covered hill in the very heart of the summer community. In Anchor Harbor, however, the poets' corner and the watering place were akin. Each was clouded in the haze of unreality that hung so charmingly over the entire peninsula. It was indeed a world unto itself. Blue, gray and green, the pattern repeated itself up and down, from the sky to the rocky mountaintops, from the sloping pine woods to the long cliffs and gleaming cold of the sea. It was an Eden in which it was hard to visualize a serpent. People were never born there, nor did they die there. The elemental was left to the winter and other climes. The sun that sparkled in the cocktails under the yellow and red umbrella tables by the club pool was the same sun that dropped behind the hills in the evening, lighting up the peninsula with pink amid the pine trees. It was a land of big ugly houses, pleasant to live in, of very old and very active ladies, of hills that were called mountains, of small, quaint shops and of large, shining town cars. When in the morning I picked up the newspaper with its angry black headlines it was not so much with a sense of their tidings being false, as of their being childishly irrelevant.

By mid-September, however, the big summer houses were closed and the last trunks of their owners were rattling in vans down the main street past the swimming club to the station. The sky was more frequently overcast; there was rain and fog, and from the sea came the sharp cold breezes that told the advent of an early winter. I was staying alone in my mother-in-law's house, taking long walks on the mountains and going at night to the movies. I suppose that I was lonelier than I cared to admit for I found myself dropping into the empty swimming club before lunch and drinking a cocktail on the terrace that looked over the unfilled pool and the bay. There were not apt to be more than one or two people there, usually the sort who had to maintain a residence in Maine for tax purposes, and I was not averse to condoling with them for a few minutes each day. It was on a day when I had not found even one of these that a youngish-looking man, perhaps in his early thirties, approached the table where I was sitting. He was an oddly shaped and odd-looking person, wide in the hips and narrow in the shoulders, and his face, very white and round and smooth, had, somewhat inconsistently, the uncertain dignity of a thin aquiline nose and large owl-like eyes. His long hair was parted in the middle and plastered to his head with a heavy tonic, and he was wearing, alas, a bow tie, a red blazer, and white flannels, a combination which was even then out of date except for sixth-form graduations at schools such as mine. All this was certainly unprepossessing, and I shrank a bit as he approached me, but there was in his large gray eyes as they gazed timidly down at me a look of guilelessness, of cautious friendliness, of anticipated rebuff that made me suddenly smile.

"My name is Gregory Bakewell. People call me Greg," he said in a mild, pleasant voice less affected than I would have anticipated. "I hope you'll excuse my intrusion, but could you tell me if they're going to continue the buffet lunch next week?"

I looked at him with a feeling of disappointment.

"I don't know," I said. "I never lunch here."

He stared with blinking eyes.

"But you ought. It's quite delicious."

I shrugged my shoulders, but he remained, obviously concerned at what I was passing up.

"Perhaps you will join me for lunch today," he urged. "It's *suprême de volaille argentée*."

I couldn't repress a laugh at his fantastic accent, and then to cover it up and to excuse myself for not lunching with him I asked him to have a drink. He sat down, and I introduced myself. I confess that I expected that he might have heard of me, and I looked into his owl eyes for some hint that he was impressed. There was none.

"You weren't up here during the season?" he asked. "You've just come?"

"That's right."

He shook his head.

"It's a pity you missed it. They say it was very gay."

I murmured something derogatory in general about the summer life at Anchor Harbor.

"You don't like it?" he asked.

"I can't abide it. Can you?"

"Me?" He appeared surprised that anyone should be interested in his reaction. "I don't really know. Mother and I go out so little. Except, of course, to the Bishop's. And dear old Mrs. Stone's."

I pictured him at a tea party, brushed and combed and wearing a bib. And eating an enormous cookie.

"I used to go out," I said.

"And now you don't?"

Even if he had never heard of me I was surprised, at Anchor Harbor, that he should not have heard of my wife. Ordinarily, I hope, I would not have said what I did say, but my need for communication was strong. I was suddenly and oddly determined to imprint my ego on the empty face of all that he took for granted.

"My wife died here," I said. "Last summer."

He looked even blanker than before, but gradually an expression of embarrassment came over his face.

"Oh, dear," he said. "I'm so sorry. Of course, if I'd known —"

I felt ashamed of myself.

"Of course," I said hurriedly. "Forgive me for mentioning it."

"But no," he protested. "I should have known. I remember now. They were speaking of her at Mrs. Stone's the other day. She was very beautiful, wasn't she?"

She hadn't been, but I nodded. I wanted even the sympathy that he could give me and swallowed greedily the small drops that fell from his meager supply.

"And which reminds me," he said, after we had talked in this vein for several minutes, "they spoke of you, too. You write things, don't you? Stories?"

I swallowed.

"I hope not," I said. "I'm an historian."

"Oh, that must be lovely."

I wondered if there was another man in the world who could have said it as he said it. He conveyed a sense of abysmal ignorance, but of humility, too, and of boundless admiration. These things were fine, were wonderful, he seemed to say, but he, too, had his little niche and a nice one, and he as well as these things existed, and we could be friends together, couldn't we?

I decided we were getting nowhere.

"What do you do?" I asked.

"Do?" Again he looked blank. "Why, good heavens, man, I don't do a thing."

I looked severe.

"Shouldn't you?"

"Should I?"

"You haven't got a family or anything like that?"

He smiled happily.

"Oh, I've got 'something like that,'" he answered. "I've got Mother."

I nodded. I knew everything now.

"Do you exercise?"

"I walk from Mother's cottage to the club. It's several hundred yards."

I rose to my feet.

"Tomorrow morning," I said firmly, "I'll pick you up here at nine-thirty. We're going to climb a mountain."

He gaped at me in horror and amazement as I got up to leave him, but he was there when I came by the next morning, waiting for me, dressed exactly as he had been the day before except for a pair of spotless white sneakers and a towel, pointlessly but athletically draped around his neck. He was very grateful to me for inviting him and told me with spirit how he had always wanted to climb a mountain at Anchor Harbor. These "mountains" were none higher than a thousand feet and the trails were easy; nonetheless I decided to start him on the smallest.

He did well enough, however. He perspired profusely and kept taking off garments as we went along, piling them on his arm, and he presented a sorry figure indeed as his long hair fell over his face and as the sweat poured down his white puffy back, but he kept up and bubbled over with talk. I asked him about his life, and he told me the dismal tale of a childhood spent under the cloud of a sickly constitution. He had been, of course, an only child, and his parents, though loving, had themselves enjoyed excellent health. He had never been to school or college; he had learned whatever it was that he did know from tutors. He had never left home, which for the Bakewells had been St. Louis until the death of Mr. Bakewell and was now St. Petersburg in Florida. Greg was thirty-five and presented to me in all his clumsy innocence a perfect *tabula rasa*. His mind was a piece of blank paper, of white, dead paper, on which, I supposed, one could write whatever message one chose. He appeared to have no prejudices or snobbishnesses; he was a guileless child who had long since ceased to fret, if indeed he ever had, at the confinements of his nursery. I could only look and gape, and yet at the same time feel the responsibility of writing the first line, for he seemed to enjoy an odd, easy content in his own placid life.

We had passed beyond the tree line and were walking along the smoother rock of the summit, a sharp cool breeze blowing in our faces. It was a breathtaking view, and I turned to see what Greg's reaction would be.

"Look," he said pointing to an ungainly shingle clock tower that protruded from the woods miles below us, "you can see the roof of Mrs. Stone's house."

I exploded.

"God!" I said.

"Don't be angry with me," he said mildly. "I was just pointing something out."

I could see that decisions had to be made and steps taken.

"Look, Greg," I said. "Don't go to St. Petersburg this winter."

He stared.

"But what would Mother do?"

I dismissed his mother with a gesture.

"Stay here. By yourself. Get to know the people who live here all the year round. Read. I'll send you books."

He looked dumbfounded.

"Then you won't be here?"

I laughed.

"I've got a job, man. I'm writing a book. But you're not. Give one winter to being away from your mother and Mrs.

Stone and the Bishop, and learn to think. You won't know yourself in a year."

He appeared to regard this as not entirely a happy prognostication.

"But Mrs. Stone and the Bishop don't go to St. Petersburg," he pointed out.

"Even so," I said.

"I really don't think I could leave Mother."

I said nothing.

"You honestly think I ought to do something?" he persisted.

"I do."

"That's what Mother keeps telling me," he said dubiously.

"Well, she's right."

He looked at me in dismay.

"But what'll I do?"

"I've made one suggestion. Now it's your turn."

He sighed.

"Well, it's very hard," he said, "to know. You pick me up, and then you throw me down."

I felt some compunction at this.

"I'll write you," I said. "To St. Petersburg. You can keep me informed of your progress."

He beamed.

"Oh, that would be very kind," he said.

During the remaining two weeks of my visit to Anchor Harbor I walked with Greg almost every day, and we became friends. It was agreeable to be with someone whose admiration was unqualified. He listened to me with the utmost respect and attention and forgot everything I said a moment afterwards. But I didn't mind. It gave me a sense of ease about repeating myself; I talked of history and literature and love; I set myself up as counsel for the forces of life and argued my case at the bar of Greg's justice, pleading that the door might be opened just a crack. Yet whoever it was who represented the forces of his inertia was supplying very cogent arguments against me. I decided that it must be his mother, and I stopped at the Bakewells' one day after our walk to meet her.

Mrs. Bakewell I had made a picture of before I met her. She would be a small grim woman, always in black, mourning the husband whose existence one could never quite believe in; she would be wearing a black ribbon choker and a shiny black hat, and she would never change the weight or the quantity of her clothing, equally inappropriate for St. Petersburg or Anchor Harbor, for any such considerations as seasons or weather. I saw her thus as small, as compact, as uncompromising, because in my imagination she had had to wither to a little black stump, the hard remnants of the heaping blaze of what I visualized as her maternal possessiveness. How else could I possibly explain Gregory except in terms of such a mother? And when I did meet her each detail of her person seemed to spring up at me to justify my presupposition. She *was* a small, black figure, and she *did* wear a broad, tight choker. She was old, and she was unruffled; her large hook nose and her small eyes had about them the stillness of a hawk on a limb. When she spoke, it was with the cold calm of a convinced fanatic, and beyond the interminable details of her small talk that dealt almost exclusively with Episcopal dogma and Episcopal teas I seemed to catch the flickering light of a sixteenth-century *auto-da-fé*. But a vital element of my preconceived portrait was missing. She showed no weakness for her only child. Indeed, her attitude towards him, for all one could see, demonstrated the most commendable indifference. He had hatched from her egg and could play around the barnyard at his will. I discovered, furthermore, that, unlike her son, she had read my books.

"It's very kind of you to take time off from your work to walk with Gregory," she said to me. "I don't suppose that he can be a very stimulating companion for an historian. He never reads anything."

Gregory simply nodded as she said this. She brought it forth without severity, as a mere matter of fact.

"Reading isn't everything," I said. "It's being aware of life that counts."

She looked at me penetratingly.

"Do you think so?" she asked. "Of course, I suppose you would. It's in line with your theories. The Bishop and I were interested in what you had to say about the free will of nations in your last book."

"Did you agree with it?"

"We did not."

Gregory looked at her in dismay.

"Now, Mother," he said protestingly, "you're not going to quarrel with my new friend?"

"I'm going to say what I wish, Gregory," she said firmly, "in my own house."

No, she certainly did not spoil him. Nor could it really be said that she was possessive. It was Greg who kept reaching for apron strings in which to enmesh himself. He seemed to yearn to be dominated. He tried vainly to have her make his decisions for him, and even after she had told him, as she invariably did, that he was old enough to think things through for himself, he would, not only behind her back but to her very face, insist to those around him that she ruled him with an iron hand. If I asked him to do something, to take a walk, to go to a movie, to dine, he would nod and smile and say "I'd love to," but he would surely add, and if she was there, perhaps in a lower tone, behind his hand: "But I'll have to get back early, you know. Mother will want to hear all about it before she goes to bed." And Mrs. Bakewell, overhearing him, with her small, fixed grim smile, did not even deign to contradict.

2

During that winter, when I was working on my book in Cambridge, I forgot poor Greg almost completely, as I usually did Anchor Harbor people. They were summer figures, and I stored them away in camphor balls with my flannels. I was surprised, therefore, each time that I received a letter from him, on the stationery of a large St. Petersburg hotel, protesting in a few lines of wretched scrawl that he had really met a number of very nice people, and could I possibly come down for a visit and meet them? One of them, I remember, he thought I would like because she wrote children's plays. I wrote him one letter and sent him a Christmas card, and that, I decided, was that.

I was in a better frame of mind when I went up to Anchor Harbor towards the end of the following July to stay with my mother-in-law. I was still keeping largely to myself, but the volume of my wife's poems was finished and in the hands of the publishers, and I no longer went out of my way to spurn people. I asked my mother-in-law one afternoon while we were sitting on the porch if the Bakewells were back in Anchor Harbor.

"Yes, I saw Edith Bakewell yesterday at Mrs. Stone's,"

she said. "Such an odd, stiff woman. I didn't know you knew them."

"Was her son there?"

"Greg? Oh, yes, he's always with her. Don't tell me *he's* a friend of yours?"

"After a fashion."

"Well, there's no accounting for tastes. I can't see a thing in him, but the old girls seem to like him. I drew him as a partner the other night at the bridge table."

"Oh, does he play bridge now?"

"If you can call it that," my mother-in-law said with a sniff. "But he certainly gets around. In my set, anyway. I never go out that I don't run into him."

"Really? Last fall he knew nobody."

"And Anchor Harbor was a better place."

Little by little I became aware that my friend's increased appearances in the summer-colony world was part of some preconceived and possibly elaborate plan of social self-advancement. He was not, I realized with a mild surprise, simply floating in the brisk wake of his mother's determined spurts; he was splashing gayly down a little back water on a course that must have had the benefit of his own navigation. At the swimming club he had abandoned the lonely couch near the table of fashion magazines, where he used to wait for his mother, for the gay groups of old ladies in flowered hats who gathered daily at high noon around the umbrella tables and waited for the sun to go over the yardarm and the waiters to come hurrying with the first glad cocktail of the day. I was vaguely disgusted at all of this, though I had no reason, as I well knew, to have expected better things, but my disgust became pointed after I had twice telephoned him to ask him for a walk and twice had to listen to his protests of a previous engagement. I wondered if he fancied that his social position was now too lofty to allow of further intimacy between us, and I laughed to myself, but rather nastily, at the idea. I would have crossed him off my books irrevocably had I not met him one day when I was taking my mother-in-law to call on old Mrs. Stone. We had found her alone, sitting on the porch with her back to the view, and were making rather slow going of a conversation about one of my books when her daughter, Theodora, came in with a group of people, including Greg, who had just returned from what seemed to have been a fairly alcoholic picnic. I found myself caught, abandoned by my fleeing mother-in-law, in the throes of a sudden cocktail party.

"My God!" cried Theodora as she spotted me. "If it isn't Arnold of Rugby!"

I had always been rather a favorite of Theodora's, for she had regarded, in the light of the subsequent tragedy, her very casual friendship with my wife, of the kind that are based on childhood animosity and little more, as the deepest relationship that she had ever known. And in all seriousness it may have been. Theodora had had little time, in her four marriages, for friendships with women. At the moment she was in one of her brief husbandless periods, and her energy, unrestrained, swept across the peninsula like a forest fire. She drew me aside, out on the far end of the huge porch, hugging my arm as she did when she had had one drink too many and hissed in my ear, with the catlike affection that purported to be a caricature of itself and which, presumably, a minimum of four men had found attractive:

"Isn't he precious?"

"Who?"

"Little Gregory, of course." And she burst into a laugh. "He tells me that you were kind to him. Great big you!"

"Where on earth did you pick him up?"

"Right here." She indicated the porch. "Right here at Mummie's. I found him in the teapot. The old bitches were stuffing him into it, as if he were the dormouse, poor precious, so I hustled right over and caught him by the fanny and pulled and pulled till he came out with a pop. And now he's mine. All mine. You can't have him."

I glanced over to where Gregory was talking to two women in slacks. His white flannels looked a tiny bit dirtier, and he was holding a cocktail rather self-consciously in his round white hand.

"I'm not sure I want him," I said gravely. "You seem to have spoiled him already."

"Oh, precious," she said, cuddling up to me. "Do you think Theodora would do that?"

"Is he to be Number Five?"

She looked up at me with her wide serious eyes.

"But could he be, darling? I mean, after all, what sex is he? Or *is* he?"

I shrugged my shoulders.

"How much does that matter at our age, Theodora?"

She was, as always, a good sport. She threw back her head and howled with laughter.

"Oh, it matters!" she exclaimed. "I tell you what, darling. Greg will be Number Seven. Or maybe even Number Six. But not the next one. No, dear. Not the next one."

I found it in me to speculate if I had not perhaps been selected on the spot for that dubious honor. Anyway, I decided to go. Conversation with Theodora who believed so patently, so brazenly, in nothing and nobody, always made me nervous. As I re-entered the house and was crossing the front hall I heard my name called. It was Greg. He ran after me and caught me by the arm at the front door.

"You're leaving!" he protested. "And you haven't even spoken to me!"

"I'm speaking to you now," I said shortly.

To my dismay he sat down on the stone bench under the portecochère and started to cry. He did not cry loudly or embarrassingly; his chest rose and fell with quiet, orderly sobs.

"My God, man!" I exclaimed.

"I knew you were mad at me," he whimpered, "by the way you spoke on the telephone when I couldn't go on a walk with you. But I didn't know you wouldn't even speak to me when you saw me!"

"I'm sorry," I said fretfully.

"You don't know what you've meant to me," he went on dolefully, rubbing his eyes. "You have no idea. You're the first person who ever asked me to do anything in my whole life. When you asked me to go for a walk with you. Last summer."

"Well, I did this summer too."

"Yes," he said, shaking his head, "I know. And I couldn't go. But the reason I couldn't go was that I was busy. And the reason I was busy was what you told me."

I stared down at him.

"What the hell did I tell you?"

"To do things. See people. Be somebody." He looked up at me now with dried eyes. There was suddenly and quite unexpectedly almost a note of confidence in his tone.

"And how do you do that?"

"The only way I can. I go out."

I ran my hand through my hair in a confusion of reluctant amusement and despair.

"I didn't mean it that way, Greg," I protested. "I wanted you to see the world. Life. Before it was too late."

He nodded placidly.

"That's what I'm doing," he said.

"But I wanted you to read big books and think big thoughts," I said desperately. "How can you twist that into my telling you to become a tea caddy?"

His wide thoughtless eyes were filled with reproach.

"You knew I couldn't read books," he said gravely. "Or think big thoughts. You were playing with me."

I stared.

"Then why did you think you had to do anything?"

"Because you made me want to." He looked away, across the gravel, into the deep green of the forest. "I could feel your contempt. I had never felt that before. No one had ever cared enough to feel contempt. Except you."

As I looked at him I wondered if there were any traces of his having felt such a sting. I was baffled, almost angry at his very expressionlessness. That he could sit and indict me so appallingly for my interference, could face me with so direct a responsibility, was surely a dreadful thing if he cared, but if he didn't, if he was simply making a fool of me . . .

"I hope you don't think," I said brutally, "that you can lessen any contempt that you think I may feel for you by becoming a social lion in Anchor Harbor."

He shook his head.

"No," he said firmly. "Your contempt is something I shall have to put up with. No matter what I do. I can't read or think or talk the way you do. I can't work. I can't even cut any sort of figure with the girls. There aren't many things open to me. You're like my mother. You know that, really, but you think of me as if I was somebody else."

I took a cigarette out of my case, lit it and sat down beside him. From around the corner of the big house came a burst of laughter from Theodora's friends.

"Where are you headed, then, Greg?" I asked him as sympathetically as I could.

He turned and faced me.

"To the top of the peninsula," he said. "I'm going to be a social leader."

I burst into a rude laugh.

"The *arbiter elegantiarum* of Anchor Harbor?" I cried.

"I don't know what that means," he said gravely.

Again I laughed. The sheer inanity of it had collapsed my mounting sympathy.

"You're mad," I said sharply. "You haven't got money or looks or even wit. Your bridge is lousy. You play no sports. Let's face it, man. You'll never make it. Even in this crazy place."

Greg seemed in no way perturbed by my roughness. His humility was complete. The only thing, I quickly divined, that could arouse the flow of his tears was to turn from him. As long as one spoke to him, one could say anything.

"Everything you say is true," he conceded blandly. "I'd be the last to deny it. But you watch. I'll get there."

"With the old ladies, perhaps," I said scornfully. "If that's what you want."

"I have to start with the old ladies," he said. "I don't know anyone else."

"And after the old ladies?"

But he had thought this out.

"They all have daughters or granddaughters," he explained. "Like Theodora. They'll get used to me."

"And you're 'cute,'" I said meanly. "You're a 'dear.' Yes, I see it. If it's what you want." I got up and started across the gravel to my car. He came after me.

"I'm not going to hurt anyone, you know," he said. "I only want to be a respected citizen."

In the car I leaned out to speak to him.

"Suppose I tell them?"

"About my plans?"

"What else?"

"Do. It won't make any difference. You'll see."

I started the motor and drove off without so much as nodding to him.

3

Gregory was good to his word. Every ounce of energy in his small store was directed to the attainment of his clearly conceived goal. I had resolved in disgust to have no further dealings with him, and I adhered to my resolution, but curiosity and a sense of the tiny drama latent in his plans kept me during the rest of that summer and the following two with an ear always alert at the mention of his name for further details of his social clamber.

Little by little Anchor Harbor began to take note of the emergence of this new personality. Greg had been right to start with the old ladies, though he had had, it was true, no alternative. The appearance of this bland young man with such innocent eyes and wide hips and such ridiculous blazers would have been followed by brusque repulse in any young or even middle-aged group of the summer colony, intent as they were on bridge, liquor, sport and sex. In the elderly circles, however, Greg had only to polish his bridge to the point of respectability, and he became a welcome addition at their dinner parties. His conversation, though certainly tepid, was soothing and enthusiastic, and he could listen, without interrupting, to the longest and most frequently repeated anecdote. He liked everybody and every dinner; he radiated an unobtrusive but gratifying satisfaction with life. Once he became known as a person who could be counted upon to accept, his evenings were gradually filled. The old in Anchor Harbor had an energy that put their descendants to shame. Dinner parties even in the septagenarian group were apt to last till two in the morning, and in the bridge circles rubber would succeed rubber until the sun peeked in through the blinds to cast a weird light on the butt-filled ash trays and the empty, sticky highball glasses. The old were still up when the young came in from their more hectic but less prolonged evenings of enjoyment, and Gregory came gradually, in the relaxed hours of the early morning, to meet the children and grandchildren of his hostesses. Friction, however, often ran high between the generations, even at such times, and he found his opportunity as peacemaker. He came to be noted for his skill in transmitting messages, with conciliatory amendments of his own, from mother to daughter, from aunt to niece. Everyone found him useful. He became in short a "character," accepted by all ages, and in that valuable capacity immune from criticism. He was "dear old Greg," "our lovable, ridiculous Greg." One heard more and more such remarks as, "Where but in Anchor Harbor would you find a type like Greg?" and "You know, I *like* Greg." And, I suppose, even had none of the foregoing been true, he would have succeeded as Theodora's pet, her "discovery," her lap dog, if you will, a comfortable, consoling eunuch in a world that had produced altogether too many men.

That Mrs. Bakewell would have little enough enthusiasm for her son's being taken to the hearts of Theodora and her set I was moderately sure, but the extent of her animosity I was not to learn until I came across her one hot August afternoon at the book counter of the stationery store which was a meeting place second only in importance to the club. She was standing very stiffly but obviously intent upon the pages of a large volume of Dr. Fosdick. She looked up in some bewilderment when I greeted her.

"I was just looking," she said. "I don't want anything, thank you."

I explained that I was not the clerk.

"I'm sorry," she said without embarrassment. "I didn't recognize you."

"Well, it's been a long time," I admitted. "I only come here for short visits."

"It's a very trivial life, I'm afraid."

"Mine? I'm afraid so."

"No," she said severely and without apology. "The life up here."

"Greg seems to like it."

She looked at me for a moment. She did not smile.

"They're killing him," she said.

I stared.

"They?"

"That wicked woman. And her associates." She looked back at her book. "But I forgot. You're of the new generation. My adjective was anachronistic."

"I liked it."

She looked back at me.

"Then save him."

"But, Mrs. Bakewell," I protested. "People don't *save* people at Anchor Harbor."

"More's the pity," she said dryly.

I tried to minimize it.

"Greg's all right," I murmured. "He's having a good time."

She closed the book.

"Drinking the way he does?"

"Does he drink?"

"Shockingly."

I shrugged my shoulders. When people like Mrs. Bakewell used the word it was hard to know if they meant an occasional cocktail or a life of confirmed dipsomania.

"And that woman?" she persevered. "Do you approve of her?"

"Oh, Mrs. Bakewell," I protested earnestly. "I'm sure there's nothing wrong between him and Theodora."

She looked at me, I thought, with contempt.

"I was thinking of their souls," she said. "Good day, sir."

I discovered shortly after this awkward interchange that there was a justification in her remarks about Greg's drinking. I went one day to a large garden party given by Mrs. Stone. All Anchor Harbor was there, old and young, and Theodora's set, somewhat contemptuous of the throng and present, no doubt, only because of Theodora, who had an odd conventionality about attending family parties, were clustered in a group near the punch bowl and exploding periodically in loud laughs. They were not laughing, I should explain, at the rest of us, but at something white-flanneled and adipose in their midst, something with a blank face and strangely bleary eyes. It was Greg, of course, and he was telling them a story, stammering and repeating himself as he did so to the great enjoyment of the little group. It came over me gradually as I watched him that Mrs. Bakewell was right. They *were* killing him. Their laughter was as cold and their acclaim as temporary as that of any audience in the arena of Rome or Constantinople. They could clap hands and cheer, they could spoil their favorites, but they could turn their thumbs down, too, and could one doubt for a moment that at the first slight hint of deteriorating performance, they would? I felt a chill in my veins as their laughter came to me again across the lawn and as I caught sight of the small, spare, dignified figure of Greg's mother standing on the porch with the Bishop and surveying the party with eyes that said nothing. If there were Romans to build fires, *there* was a martyr worthy of their sport. But Gregory. Our eyes suddenly met, and I thought I could see the appeal in them; I thought I could feel his plea for rescue flutter towards me in my isolation through the golden air of the peninsula. Was that why his mother had come? As I turned to her I thought that she, too, was looking at me.

He had left his group. He was coming over to me.

"Well?" I said.

"Come over and meet these people," he said to me, taking me by the arm. "Come on. They're charming." He swayed slightly as he spoke.

I shook my arm loose.

"I don't want to."

He looked at me with his mild, steady look.

"Please," he urged.

"I said no," I snapped. "Why should I want to clutter my

summer with trash like that? Go on back to them. Eat garbage. You like it."

He balanced for a moment on the balls of his feet. Evidently he regarded my violence as something indigenous to my nature and to be ignored.

"Theodora's never been in better form," he held out to me as bait.

"Good for Theodora," I said curtly. "And in case you don't know it, you're drunk."

He shook his head sadly at me and wandered slowly back to his group.

4

Gregory went from glory to glory. He became one of the respected citizens of the summer colony. His spotless white panama was to be seen bobbing on the bench of judges at the children's swimming meet. He received the prize two years running for the best costume at the fancy dress ball. On each occasion he went as a baby. He was a sponsor of the summer theater, the outdoor concerts, and the putting tournament. He was frequently seated on the right of his hostess at the very grandest dinners. He arrived early in the season and stayed into October. What he did during the winter months was something of a mystery, but it was certain that he did not enjoy elsewhere a success corresponding to his triumph at Anchor Harbor. Presumably, like so many Anchor Harbor people whose existence away from the peninsula it was so difficult to conceive, he went into winter hibernation to rest up for his exhausting summers.

That he continued to drink too much when he went out, which was, of course, all the time, did not, apparently, impair his social position. He was firmly entrenched, as I have said, in his chosen category of "character," and to these much is allowed. Why he drank I could only surmise. It might have been to steady himself in the face of a success that was as unnerving as it was unfamiliar; it might have been to make him forget the absurdity of his ambitions and the hollowness of their fulfillment, or it might even have been to shelter himself from the bleak wind of his mother's reproach. Theodora and all her crowd drank a great deal. It was possible that he had simply picked up the habit from them. It would have gone unnoticed, at least in that set, had it not been for a new and distressing habit that he had developed, of doing, after a certain number of drinks, a little dance by himself, a sort of jig, that was known as "Greg's peg." At first he did it only for a chosen few, late at night, amid friendly laughter, but word spread, and the little jig became an established feature of social life on Saturday night dances at the club. There would be a roll of drums, and everybody would stop dancing and gather in a big circle while the sympathetic orchestra beat time to the crazy marionette in the center. Needless to say I had avoided being a witness of "Greg's peg," but my immunity was not to last.

It so happened that the first time that I was to see this sordid performance was the last time that it ever took place. It was on a Saturday night at the swimming-club dance, the festivity that crowned the seven-day madness known as "tennis week," the very height, mind you, of Anchor Harbor's dizzy summer of gaiety. Even my mother-in-law and I had pulled ourselves sufficiently together to ask a few friends for dinner and take them on to the club. We found the place milling with people and a very large band playing very loudly. I noticed several young men who were not in evening dress and others whose evening clothes had obviously been borrowed, strong, ruddy, husky young men. It was the cruise season, and the comfortable, easy atmosphere of overdressed but companionable Anchor Harbor was stiffened by an infiltration of moneyed athleticism and arrogance from the distant smartness of Long Island and Newport. All throbbed, however, to the same music, and all seemed to be enjoying themselves. Theodora, in a sweater and pleated skirt and large pearls, dressed to look as though she were off a sailboat and not, as she was, fresh from her own establishment, spotted me and with characteristic aplomb deserted her partner and came over to our table. She took in my guests with an inclusive, final and undiscriminating smile that might have been a greeting or a shower of alms, took a seat at the table and monopolized me.

"Think of it," she drawled. "You at a dance. What's happened? Well, anyway," she continued without waiting for my answer, "I approve. See life. Come for lunch tomorrow. Will you? Two o'clock. I'll have some people who might amuse you."

Since her mother's death Theodora had begun to take on the attributes of queen of the peninsula. She dealt out her approval and disapproval as if it was possible that somebody cared. Struggling behind the wall of her make-up, her mannerisms and her marriages one could sense the real Theodora, strangled at birth, a dowager, with set lips and outcasting frown, a figure in pearls for an opera box. I declined her invitation and asked if Gregory was going to do his dance.

"Oh, the darling," she said huskily. "Of course, he will.

I'll get hold of him in a minute and shoo these people off the floor."

"Don't do it for me," I protested. "I don't want to see it. I hear it's a disgusting sight."

She snorted.

"Whoever told you that?" she retorted. "It's the darling's precious little stunt. Wait till you see it. Oh, I know you don't like him," she continued wagging her finger at me. "He's told me that enough times, the poor dear. You've hurt him dreadfully. You pretend you can't stand society when the only thing you can't stand is anything the least bit unconventional."

I wondered if this were not possibly true. She continued to stare at me from very close range. It was always impossible to tell if she was drunk or sober.

"Like his old bitch of a mother," she continued.

"That's a cruel thing to say, Theodora," I protested sharply. "Do you even know her?"

"Certainly I know her. She's sat on poor Greg all his life. Lord knows what dreadful things she did to him when he was a child."

"Greg told you this?"

"He never complains, poor dear. But I'm no fool. I can read between the lines."

"If she's a bitch you know what that makes him," I said stiffly. "I was going to ask you tonight to give him back to his mother. She's the one person who knows what you're doing to him. But now I don't want to. It's too late. Keep him. Finish the dirty job."

"You must be drunk," she said and left me.

It was not long after this that the orchestra suddenly

struck up a monotonous little piece with a singsong refrain and as at a concerted signal the couples on the floor gathered in a half-circle around the music, leaving a space in which something evidently was going on. The non-Anchor Harborites on the floor did not know what it was all about, but they joined with the others to make an audience for the diversion. I could see nothing but backs from where I was sitting, and suddenly hearing the laughter and applause and an odd tapping sound, I was overcome with curiosity and, taking my mother-in-law, we hurried across the dance floor and peered between the heads that barred our view.

What I saw there I shall never be able to get out of my mind. In the center of the half-circle formed by the crowd Gregory was dancing his dance. His eyes were closed and his long hair, disarrayed, was streaked down over his sweating face. His mouth, half open, emitted little snorts as his feet capered about in a preposterous jig that could only be described as an abortive effort at tap dancing. His arms moved back and forth as if he were striding along; his head was thrown back; his body shimmied from side to side. It was not really a dance at all; it was a contortion, a writhing. It looked more as if he were moving in a doped sleep or twitching at the end of a gallows. The lump of pallid softness that was his body seemed to be responding for the first time to his consciousness; it was only thus, after all, that the creature could use it. I turned in horror from the drunken jigger to his audience and noted the laughing faces, heard with disgust the "Go it, Greg!" It was worse now than the hysterical arena; it had all the obscenity of a strip-tease.

As I turned back to the sight of Gregory, his eyes opened, and I think he saw me. I thought for a second that once again I could make out the agonized appeal, but again I may have been wrong. It seemed to me that his soul, over which Mrs. Bakewell had expressed such concern, must have been as his body, white and doughy, possessed of no positive good and no positive evil, but a great passive husk on which the viri of the latter, once settled, could tear away. I turned to my mother-in-law who shared my disgust; we were about to go back to our table when I heard, behind us, snatches of a conversation from a group that appeared to feel even more strongly than we did. Looking back, I saw several young men in flannels and tweed coats, obviously from a cruise.

"Who the hell is that pansy?"

"Did you ever see the like of it?"

"Oh, it's Anchor Harbor. They're all that way."

"Let's throw him in the pool."

"Yes!"

I recognized one of them as a graduate of my school. I took him aside.

"Watch out for your friends, Sammy," I warned him. "Don't let them touch him. Remember. This is his club and not yours. And every old lady on the peninsula will be after you to tear your eyes out."

He nodded.

"Yes, sir. Thank you."

This may have kept Sammy under control, but his friends were another matter. When Greg had finished his jig and just as general dancing was about to be resumed, four young men stepped up to him and quietly lifted him in the air, perching him on the shoulders of two of their number. They then proceeded to carry him around the room. This was interpreted as a sort of triumphal parade, as though students were unhorsing and dragging a prima donna's carriage through enthusiastic streets, and everybody applauded vociferously while Greg, looking rather dazed, smiled and fluttered his handkerchief at the crowd. Even I, forewarned, was concluding that it was all in good fun when suddenly the four young men broke into a little trot and scampered with their burden out onto the porch, down the flagstone steps and across the patch of lawn with the umbrella tables to where the long pool shimmered under the searchlights on the clubhouse roof. People surged out on the terrace to watch them; I rushed out myself and got there just in time to see the four young men, two holding the victim's arms and two his legs, swinging him slowly back and forth at the edge of the pool. There was a moment of awful silence; then I heard Theodora's shriek, and several ladies rushed across the lawn to stop them. It was too late. There was a roar from the crowd as Greg was suddenly precipitated into the air. He hung there for a split second in the glare of the searchlights, his hair flying out; then came the loud splash as he disappeared. A moment later he reappeared and burbled for help. There were shouts of "He can't swim" and at least three people must have jumped in after him. He was rescued and restored to a crowd of solicitous ladies in evening dress who gathered at the edge of the pool to receive him in their arms, regardless of his wetness. At this point I turned to go. I had no wish to see the four young men lynched. I heard later that they managed to escape with their skins and to their boats. They did not come back.

5

Gregory appeared to have developed nothing but a bad cold from the mishap. He spent the next two days in his bed, and the driveway before his mother's little cottage was jammed with tall and ancient Lincoln and Pierce-Arrow town cars bringing flowers from his devoted friends. When he recovered Theodora gave a large lunch for him at the club. Everybody was very kind. But it became apparent after a little that, however trivial the physical damage may have been, something in the events of that momentous evening had impaired the native cheerfulness of Greg's sunny disposition. On Saturday nights he could no longer be prevailed upon to do his little dance, and at high noon his presence was frequently missed under the umbrella tables when the waiters in scarlet coats came hurrying with the first Martini of the day. Theodora even spread the extraordinary news that he was thinking of going with his mother to Cape Cod the following summer. He had told her that the pace at Anchor Harbor was bad for his heart.

"That old witch of a mother has got her claws back into him," she told me firmly. "Mark my words. You'll see."

But I suspected that even Greg could see what I could see, that despite the sympathy and the flowers, despite the public outcry against the rude young men, despite the appeal in every face that things would again and always be as they had been before, despite all this, he had become "poor Greg." What had happened to him was not the sort of thing that happened to other people. When all was said and done, he may have known, as I knew, that in the last analysis even Theodora was on the side of the four young men. And perhaps he did realize it, for he was never heard to complain. Silently he accepted the verdict, if verdict it was, and disappeared early that September with his mother to St. Petersburg. I never head of him again until several years later I chanced to read of his death of a heart attack in Cape Cod. I asked some friends of mine who spent the summer there if they had ever heard of him. Only one had. He said that he remembered Greg as a strange pallid individual who was to be seen in the village carrying a basket during his mother's marketing. She had survived him, and her mourning, if possible, was now a shade darker than before.

THE END